Birk Carried His New Bride Into The Bridal Tepee.

He placed Lacey on her feet and looked at her. She held her breath as Birk's long, slow look took in the traditional Tallchief bridal outfit—the beaded doeskin shift and beaded moccasins.

Birk's hands cradled her cheeks, and he said, "You're perfect, Lacey."

"It's just like you to say something like that now. Why couldn't you stick to—" she began as a tear slid down her cheek.

"Because you are," he said in the same firm tone he'd used when he'd taken his vows on the wind-kissed knoll on Tallchief Mountain. He shouldn't have kissed her as if he'd give her all the days of his life. He shouldn't have tasted of kept promises and tomorrows. He shouldn't have been the perfect picture of a groom candidate, but he was....

Dear Reader,

This month: strong and sexy heroes!

First, the Tallchiefs—that intriguing, legendary family—are back, and this time it's Birk Tallchief who meets his match in Cait London's MAN OF THE MONTH, *The Groom Candidate*. Birk's been pining for Lacey MacCandliss for years, but once he gets her, there's nothing but trouble of the most *romantic* kind. Don't miss this delightful story from one of Desire's most beloved writers.

Next, nobody creates a strong, sexy hero quite like Sara Orwig, and in her latest, *Babes in Arms*, she brings us Colin Whitefeather, a tough and tender man you'll never forget. And in Judith McWilliams's *Another Man's Baby* we meet Philip Lysander, a Greek tycoon who will do anything to save his family…even pretend to be a child's father.

Peggy Moreland's delightful miniseries, TROUBLE IN TEXAS, continues with *Lone Star Kind of Man*. The man in question is rugged rogue cowboy Cody Fipes. In *Big Sky Drifter*, by Doreen Owens Malek, a wild Wyoming man named Cal Winston tames a lonely woman. And in Cathie Linz's *Husband Needed*, bachelor Jack Elliott surprises himself when he offers to trade his single days for married nights.

In Silhouette Desire you'll always find the most irresistible men around! So enjoy!

Lucia Macro

Senior Editor

Please address questions and book requests to:
Silhouette Reader Service
U.S.: 3010 Walden Ave., P.O. Box 1325, Buffalo, NY 14269
Canadian: P.O. Box 609, Fort Erie, Ont. L2A 5X3

CAIT LONDON
THE GROOM CANDIDATE

SILHOUETTE *Desire*®
Published by Silhouette Books
America's Publisher of Contemporary Romance

To Lana and Tom Davis.

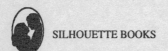

SILHOUETTE BOOKS

ISBN 0-373-76093-0

THE GROOM CANDIDATE

Books by Cait London

Silhouette Desire

The Loving Season #502
Angel vs. MacLean #593
The Pendragon Virus #611
The Daddy Candidate #641
†Midnight Rider #726
The Cowboy #763
Maybe No, Maybe Yes #782
†The Seduction of Jake Tallman #811
Fusion #871
The Bride Says No #891
Mr. Easy #919
Miracles and Mistletoe #968
‡The Cowboy and the Cradle #1006
‡Tallchief's Bride #1021
‡The Groom Candidate #1093

Silhouette Yours Truly

Every Girl's Guide To...
Every Groom's Guide To...

Silhouette Books

‡Tallchief for Keeps
Spring Fancy 1994
"Lightfoot and Loving"

*The MacLeans
†The Blaylocks
‡The Tallchiefs

CAIT LONDON

lives in the Missouri Ozarks but loves to travel the Northwest's gold rush/cattle drive trails every summer. She loves research trips, meeting people and going to Native American dances. Ms. London is an avid reader who loves to paint, play with computers and grow herbs—particularly scented geraniums right now. She's a national bestselling and award-winning author, and she also writes historical romances under another pseudonym. Three is her lucky number; she has three daughters, and the events in her life have always been in threes. "I love writing for Silhouette," she says. "One of the best perks about all this hard work is the thrilling reader response and the warm, snug sense that I have given readers an enjoyable, entertaining gift."

Duncan m. Sybil   Calum m. Talia   Birk m. Lacey   Elspeth m. Alek   Fiona
        | |
      Emily   Kira
        |
      Megan

Legends of the Tallchiefs

Duncan—The woman who brings the cradle to a man of Fearghus blood will fill it with his babies.

Calum—When a man of Fearghus blood places the ring upon the right woman's finger, he'll capture his true love forever.

Elspeth—When the Marrying Moon is high, a scarred warrior will rise from the mists to claim his lady huntress. He will wrap her in the shawl and carry her to the Bridal Tepee and his heart. Their song will last longer than the stars.

Birk—The maiden who rocks upon the chair and sings a lullaby will claim the man of Fearghus blood who stands closest to her. She will be his heart and he will be her love.

THE TALLCHIEFS

Prologue

"It's my fault that man shot your folks, isn't it?" Ten-year-old Lacey MacCandliss peered from the night at Birk. The back porch light of the Tallchiefs' ranch home outlined her small body, draped in a quilt and almost swallowed by the cold October mist.

The wind curled around Birk, rustling the leaves at his boots and reminding him that his parents had been killed. At sixteen years old, and fighting his need to cry, Birk slammed the chopping ax into the stump. "Go home, half-pint."

His hands ached, raw with blisters despite the leather gloves he'd been wearing. The mountain of chopped wood had grown in the five days since Birk's parents had been killed in a convenience store robbery.

The Tallchiefs were the only ones who could have tracked the killer into the mountains at night, a skill they had learned from their father and one passed down from their great-great-grandfather, a Sioux chieftain. The sheriff had waited until dawn on the morning after the killing, but the Tallchief brothers—Duncan, Calum and Birk—had set out at once on horseback. No one had stopped them, because the Tallchiefs were the best trackers. Just fourteen years old, Elspeth had stiffened her back and kept her hand on ten-year-old Fiona, keeping her safe as the Tallchief brothers rode into the mountains, shielded by the night. At eighteen, Duncan was the eldest, then Calum—a year younger, and Birk. They returned, their faces hard, and the killer had wept before the sheriff, glad to be out of their hands. Birk didn't feel like "Birk the rogue" now; he felt old and drained.

Birk ripped off his gloves and glanced at the rugged peaks behind Tallchief Cattle Ranch. In the Rocky Mountains, one mountain had been claimed by his family. Up on Tallchief Mountain, his parents rested and soon would be covered with a blanket of snow.

Birk stood, legs wide and braced against the wind. He stared at the raw places on his hands, caught by the pain in his heart.

Small hands slid into his and he looked down to see Lacey's pale face, her wide blue eyes shimmering with tears. One fattened and fell to his palm, shimmering in it. The same age as Fiona, Lacey had seen more than her years, thanks to her parents. Her lips trembled and yet she clung to his hands when Birk would have drawn away— after all, he was a guy, he couldn't be holding hands with a kid and letting her see that he was shattered....

"It was me, wasn't it? I told you that Ma said I didn't need pizza and that I was fat enough already. You probably told your Ma and—"

"Lay off." Birk watched Lacey recoil from his sharp tone, as if taking a slap. But she was right. He had asked his mother to buy pizza—the specialty of the convenience store—because Lacey had never had the best pizza in miles. Unless Lacey ate at the Tallchief table, she rarely had decent food. Birk wouldn't have her battered with guilt; he was carrying enough of his own. "Hey, kid. Lay off. I wanted pizza for myself, got it?"

Her fingers were freezing, so small and pale against his own. Lacey was wearing Fiona's old coat and a big woolen neck scarf that Elspeth had woven. Her fingers held his hands tightly, her big eyes searching his and finding the devastation of his heart. "I love you, Birk," she whispered tremulously.

Birk managed a, "Yeah, kid. I love you, too."

He couldn't let go of those small fingers clinging to his. "It's night and miles from town. It's freezing. How did you get here?"

"Rode my bike. It works fine, since you fixed it for me. I got this great coat of Fiona's and the scarf Elspeth wove for me, and over it all, I wrapped up warm in the quilt your Ma made me—" Lacey's lips trembled and she dashed away the tears flowing down her cheeks. "Don't you tell me to go away, Birk Tallchief. Don't you dare. I came to pay my respects, 'cause that's the right thing to do, and my Ma wouldn't bring me. Anyway, Ma is 'entertaining' now and told me to get lost. Ma says you'll go to separate foster homes now, except for Duncan and he'll lose the ranch."

"Is that so?" Birk asked tightly. His mother had wanted to protect Lacey, to bring her into the Tallchief family. But Lacey's pride and her unshakable allegiance to her mother had stopped Pauline Tallchief, a former judge.

Birk pushed back his fear that the Tallchiefs could be separated. He looked at the too-small girl holding his hands and said confidently, "That won't happen. We're staying together, here, same as always."

She shivered, her face luminous with cold and fear. She peered down at his abused hands, touched the opened blisters with the tip of one small finger.

He needed this bit of a girl, despite his pride. Birk swiped the back of his hand across the tears on his cheeks.

"Hold me—I'm cold." She held up her thumb, a tiny scar crossing the tip. "See? I'm wearing the Tallchief blood sister sign. I'm one of you, or almost."

Birk glanced at the house and decided that if no one saw him, he might hold the girl on his lap. She was just the same as Fiona, and needing warmth and comfort. When he had time, he'd take care of Jo MacCandliss, because his mother would have wanted Lacey to be protected. Birk allowed the girl to hold his hand while he sat in the old rocking chair on the back porch.

Lacey plopped herself in his lap, startling Birk. She glared at him. "Don't let me scare you, bub. Your dad held me on his lap, and Duncan and Calum, too. Tell me how you know you'll be safe, so's I won't have to worry about it.... I just don't have the heart to worry about more things. Aye, I would worry."

When the Tallchiefs said "Aye" it was a pledge and Birk nodded. Birk stared at her, this child too old for her years. He had to believe her, to believe in himself and the Tallchiefs. "I chose my great-great-grandmother Una Fearghus's rocking chair to find and return to our family as my pledge. It's in her journals, how Tallchief captured her—an indentured servant. Before that part of her dowry was sold to keep Tallchief land, Una sat in the chair and rocked her babies in it. Here goes—*The maiden who rocks upon the chair and sings a lullaby will claim the man of Fearghus blood who stands closest to her. She will be his heart and he will be her love.*"

"I'll be your love, Birk."

"Sure you will, kid."

One

"Lacey MacCandliss has finally ruined me for life," Birk muttered as he ladled another gourd-dipper of water onto the sweat lodge's round, flat, heated rocks. The rocks were layered into a pit in the center of the small building. Steam boiled and hissed into the air, matching Birk's smoldering temper. Clouds rose to the center opening of the lodge he had built years ago, covered with birch bark, and Birk wished he could send the thought of Lacey's kiss out with the smoke. Droplets of steam settled onto Birk's nude body, mixing with his sweat. With his arms behind his head, he lay naked on a wooden bench and studied the layered bark walls, keeping in the steam.

An autumn leaf, a shimmering gold aspen, hovered in the small center hole, then drifted away on the mountain wind.

October had always stirred the Tallchiefs' personal storms, the month when their parents had stopped for pizza that fatal night. Birk inhaled sharply; he'd asked his mother for the special treat...it was to celebrate the adding of a new ram to the Tallchief flock. But it was also because Lacey MacCandliss, a scrawny, blue-eyed, hungry bit of bones and freckles, the same age as Fiona, had never tasted the best pizza in town.

The wind swept down Tallchief Mountain, a jutting stark mountain filled with sheer rock cliffs and beautiful meadows that had reminded him of his great-great-grandmother, Una, of Scotland. Leaves hit the birch bark in a sound that had comforted Birk since the first time he'd built the sweat lodge—his hideout from Lacey.

He'd come here to cleanse and meditate in the old ways, to erase the unique, enticing taste of Lacey's mouth. Properly sweating, he would run straight into the freezing waters of Tallchief Lake, shouting, and forget the disaster of her lips, soft against his. He'd shiver in the freezing mountain air and beat himself with birch branches. It was so simple, and the taste of her lips would be forgotten.

After dressing, he would saddle his Appaloosa gelding, Storm Maker, and ride down from Tallchief Mountain, cleansed of Lacey MacCandliss.

At thirty-five, Birk liked to kiss women, but not Lacey MacCandliss. Every time he came close to her, which was often because she was almost his sister and a member of the Tallchiefs, he met with disaster. The latest event occurred at Elspeth's wedding just five days ago.

Birk scowled through the steam to the tiny ash floating upward. There he was, feeling like an oversize adult orphan, circled by the legends of his great-great-grandmother and the Sioux chieftain who had captured her, all coming true. Duncan had married Sybil, fulfilling the legend of the cradle; Calum had married Talia Petrovna, and the legend of the garnet ring came true. Then Alek, Talia's brother, had come to claim Elspeth, captured by Una's paisley shawl and the Marrying Moon legend. Birk had yet to find the small rocking chair that Una's indentured family had brought to the New World, and with it, claim his legend.

Birk had tossed away that whimsy long ago. The chair

had been lost for over a century and a half, and had probably gone to kindling.

Elspeth and Alek Petrovna's wedding ceremony was almost completed when Lacey had snuggled to Birk's side, just as she did when she was a child and needing reassurance. Lacey had been too quiet and, just as he had done when they were younger, Birk sensed she needed cuddling— *Cuddling? He'd wrapped his arms around Lacey MacCandliss as if he needed her to live—he'd fitted his mouth to hers and dived into—*

"Well, hell." Birk clamped his lips closed. Lacey had him talking to himself. "The Tallchiefs are falling like flies...first Duncan, then Calum and then Elspeth. No wonder I'm delicate."

Birk tossed a small bundle of sage onto the heated rocks and let the ritualistic cleansing herb, mixed with the scent of sweetgrass curl around him. Leaning against him, Lacey had been so much a part of his life. He comforted her automatically when she leaned her head on his shoulder. Her light sob hit him like a brawling boxer's punch, leveled him, and his arm closed firmly around her, gathering her to him. He'd kissed her forehead—she was a good foot shorter than him and over eighty pounds lighter.

He'd kissed her cheek, to let her know that she was safe, just as he'd always done—until she was seventeen and getting big ideas.

He'd kissed her nose, edged aside a black wild ringlet scented with the flowers she wore in her hair. He'd moved down to capture the soft sigh upon her lips.

The sweet taste of her caught him, wound around him, and drew him closer. Her lips were soft—he slipped into heaven and heat and storms all at the same time and he ached where every slight, feminine curve touched him. Since they were both wearing the Tallchiefs' kilts to please Elspeth, good strong denim didn't shield his immediate need to bear her to the ground...or to toss her onto his horse and ride off into the mountains with her.

Birk slashed his hand across his face, flicking away his

sweat. He'd dived into the taste of Lacey and forgot that the entire town of Amen Flats and his family watched him kiss her, gripping her hair in both fists. Birk tossed more water onto the coals and shook his head grimly. He could still feel her hair—a mass of wild, untamed, long spirals tossed by the wind…like warm, living silk curling around his hands.

He'd wanted to bury himself in it, drape it around her breasts— Good Lord. *Lacey MacCandliss's small breasts!* Birk's headache pounded. "It's October. I'm a Tallchief…and any man would have kissed the woman next to him under those circumstances." He liked women, adored them—logical, feminine average-size women with sweet personalities. Lacey, at twenty-nine was none of the above. She was his worst nightmare, a tough competitor in the remodeling business and half his size.

Half his size. Birk studied the stones in the lodge's center pit and tossed on a handful of aromatic herbs, a donation of Elspeth, who knew that he'd be brooding about Lacey. Lacey hadn't felt like a child…she had fitted snugly into his arms, pasted against his body as his arms drew her closer. She was all woman and what he had been seeking….

He'd taught her how to build a dollhouse…how to drive, how to use a power saw— She was more like his sister than a desirable woman.

Birk wasn't teaching her anything more about kissing. He'd leave that to someone who didn't want to survive. Besides, in the time between her seventeenth and twenty-first years, Lacey had been known as "Racey Lacey" and had led the males in the area a frantic chase with her short, short skirts and tight jeans. An athletic, compact Venus, she'd simply worn men out with challenges, left them in her dust, and Birk didn't want to think about what else she'd used to exhaust them. She'd craved attention and men were only too happy to oblige. No lectures from the Tallchiefs had stopped her as she danced away, laughing at the games. She'd settled down…on a typical Lacey level after

Birk saved her from a near rape. He knew she unde
just what dangerous game she played, and yet—

Why had Lacey's kiss thrown him into heaven?

Birk circled his thoughts—for the past three years something had been bothering Lacey. No one else had noticed during the preparations for Elspeth's wedding, but Birk had seen Lacey's desperate shadows and storms. Until she was seventeen, he knew her better than anyone. Whatever bothered her now, she hadn't stopped taking it out on him.

He'd kissed her, tasted her! Lacey MacCandliss was everything Birk didn't want in a woman—tough, cynical, extremely competitive, and marked by scars. She didn't want children or homemaking or commitment to anything, anyone—except to torment him.

Irritated that he'd let himself think of Lacey, Birk tossed a handful of small branches, chosen for their scent, onto the coals. He reached to widen the small hole, allowing for the smoke to escape. After tugging aside the small board covering the hole, he settled down to his wooden bench.

At the wedding, he'd slid his fingers through Lacey's curling black hair to find the shape of her head, lifting her up to his level for his kiss—for just a heartbeat, Lacey MacCandliss had tasted like his dreams.

Until she kneed him in a vulnerable place. Her fist to his jaw packed more muscle than he'd expected; her leg had tangled with the back of his and...and in front of the whole town of Amen Flats, who were used to the Tallchiefs' antics, he'd sprawled to his backside.

"My damn kilt blew up," Birk muttered darkly as he remembered Lacey huffing off with a fiery, threatening look over her shoulder. With her kilt and tartan flying, she'd leaped onto that big demon she called a motorcycle, revved it up and roared off, leaving him to deal with hoots, his pain and humiliation.

Birk inhaled, forcing his thoughts into a cool, logical pattern. He was a craftsman after all, an artist at building plans and breathing life into the plans, an expert at restoring beloved furniture. He planned everything, despite his image of a carefree bachelor. *He hadn't planned that kiss.* He inhaled the fragrance of sage and sweetgrass and tried to calm himself, to push away the need to run her down and kiss her again. He was delicate, Birk repeated. After all, he'd just been dumped by another fiancée, thanks to Lacey. A man had a right to be off balance when his sister got married. He'd just held Megan, Duncan's toddler, and Calum's new baby girl, Kira, a newborn, had nestled in Birk's arms, bundled and protected by his plaid. "Burp and baby powder can be a deadly combination."

Chelsey Lang had just confronted him with the information Lacey had dropped into her lap; Chelsey really shouldn't have tried to lay down rules for him—he'd speak to whomever he wanted, including the town's bad girl— and the almost-engagement was off. For the time being, his prospects for a prospective bride were zero. Lacey's kiss had taken advantage of his current womanless state.

Lacey had taken advantage of him! he thought, outraged.

"It's October and I'm a Tallchief...I'm susceptible to weddings and babies," he noted with a cough.

His eyes burned; smoke layered the lodge, the center hole was now completely covered. He realized suddenly that he had been tossing more wood to the coals and that the fire had ignited, hurling smoke into the small, tight sweat lodge. He reached for a towel and remembered it was at the creek, waiting for him after he plunged into the icy water. Birk grabbed the boughs covering the sweat lodge's doorway and tore his way free of the smoke-filled lodge.

Freezing mountain air swept over his sweaty body. Pine boughs covered the center hole, damming the smoke; his horse and clothing were gone. Lacey's small work boots had left prints around the lodge. An expert hunter, Birk tracked her prints to where she had parked her motorcycle. She'd left him with his western boots, one sock and a brisk seven-mile walk down the mountain, through the deep, dangerous timber, to Amen Flats and Lacey's house. Birk grimly split the sock with his knife, whipped the lengthened

knit between his legs, loincloth fashion, and tied a rope
around his hips to tether it in place. He scanned the area
and found the folded grocery sacks he'd stuffed in a plastic
bag. Birk quickly fashioned the paper sacks around him,
tying them with twine, and tugged the plastic bag over it
all. He ignored the icy wind; he had his temper to keep
him warm.

Lacey MacCandliss had stalked him—him, a Tallchief
with years of tracking and camping experience. "She is
going to pay for this," he promised grimly and began lop-
ing through the woods toward Amen Flats.

Lacey wrapped her arms around her and paced through
the old bordello that she was constantly refinishing. She
didn't think of it as a "money pit," but as a home that
suited her and needed care. The original woods were the
best, the structure sturdy, and because the frontier women
of Amen Flats wouldn't have Lil's Place close by, the
house was a respectable distance from town. Outside, in the
night, across the spacious old porch, down the wide steps
and down the road were the families of Amen Flats, lights
twinkling in their homes. Lacey had a home now, not a
cold, dirty shack. She'd saved for years to buy the beautiful,
elegant house, high on a knoll, overlooking all of Amen
Flats. There was Calum and Talia's house and their two-
week-old baby, Kira, and up on Tallchief Mountain, Duncan had remodeled the old house and Sybil was seven
months into another baby. Though she was bred of Celtic
seer and Native American shaman blood, Elspeth didn't
seem aware of how she glowed—Lacey had seen enough
of "the glow" to recognize a potential pregnancy.

While she was happy for the growing Tallchief family,
Lacey wanted no children, no ties, nothing but absolute
freedom.

She'd taken scraps and pasted herself into a secure,
pleasant life that suited her. With Calum, the Tallchiefs'
business guru, helping her, Lacey had sold the old Mac-
Candliss shack. Remodeled with leftover wood and roofing

materials, the shack had made the down payment money on Lil's Place. In the seven years since she'd lived in the old bordello, she'd reroofed, torn out every wall and strengthened the substructure. Every day off was spent making this discarded house strong, like Lacey had made her life. She'd torn away the rotted wood as if it were her past, replacing it with new, strong boards.

She liked the sound of her work boots hitting solid wood boards, wide planks, with occasional rugs for her pets' comfort. She loved looking at her house—her drawing table with its lamp, and another table used for a desk. A copy of her first check for building a deck on Lisa James's mobile home was framed above it all. Her filing cabinets were stuffed with plans and contracts and payroll records. She'd built her business from nothing and now with four men as her crew, she had the remodeling contract for the church. Calum Tallchief's fine accounting skills had helped her build a bankroll and a checkbook and a—

She had a mother who had been taking payments for three years and was coming back to Amen Flats. Calum hadn't questioned her withdrawals from her account, but had asked if he could help. She'd refused him and Duncan, who managed Tallchief Cattle Ranch, the land owned by all the Tallchiefs.

Lacey realized she was clenching her fists. She felt her strength and the calluses on her hands. She could manage her mother's visit and the payments and continue as before—on her own, responsible to no one and no one taking care of her. She wasn't a seventeen-year-old kid anymore, scared and alone in a shack because her mother had deserted her.

The flowers Lacey had held at Elspeth's wedding hung upside down on the wall; there were dried wildflowers from Tallchief Mountain, herbs from Elspeth's garden, and orchids from Alek's father.

Birk had kissed her like he'd kiss a woman! She jammed firewood into the huge woodstove sitting in the middle of the spacious interior, supported by huge oak beams. Birk deserved to cool off with a naked walk through the woods, after the way he kissed her in front of the whole town. It had taken her an entire week to catch him alone and vulnerable. Bred of men who knew how to survive in the wilderness, Birk had run a winter endurance race when he was celebrating his twenty-first birthday. His bathing suit and moccasins had not lessened the savage masculine impact as he finished first of the pack. Out of breath, swaggering, and bold, Birk had been in his element, bred to it, his smile flashing at her—

Lacey wiped the back of her hand across her mouth. She'd known everything about him and yet he'd managed to surprise her…snag her with that kiss. She didn't want to think about the hunger in Birk's kiss, or the feeling that she was coming home. He shouldn't have wrapped his arms around her and lifted her to his seeking mouth. She'd heard about it, that Tallchief kiss that let few escape, that sweet, tantalizing hunger that made a woman want to—

Dressed in his kilt, there was no mistaking the hardened shape of his body.

She wouldn't be toyed with by Birk Tallchief; she'd seen him charm enough women with one dark look, one deep, throaty laugh. Late this afternoon, Birk got what he deserved, stranded at his sweat lodge without his clothes. Doris Muller had been eyeing him and if Birk took the Low Pass, she was only a good three-mile walk from the sweat lodge. He'd go there and get warm soon enough; Birk's way with women was legendary. Another mile more and there was Frannie Simmons, who had always wanted a taste of Birk Tallchief. Lacey had no one but herself, wanted no interference in her life, and— Lacey crouched to gather the cats and dogs following her into her arms.

Her mother was coming back to Amen Flats in November, just another month, and the one person Lacey had turned to for comfort shouldn't have been Birk.

Lacey squeezed her lids closed, fighting the memories that came to haunt her. Her mother's voice had been coarse, drunken— *Get in that closet and stay there!* Lacey looked at the spacious open design of her home. There were no walls, no closets now, only a cloth drape separating the bathroom.

Lacey plopped onto a stool and briskly unlaced her work boots, kicking them off. She whipped off her sweatshirt, shimmied out of her jeans, and strolled to the kitchen area, dressed in her long thermal underwear and her heavy work socks.

Her herd, a collection of cats and dogs, all mistreated orphans like herself, followed at her heels. Gizmo, a black Labrador-rottweiler yard dog bumped pleasantly against Lacey's thighs, wanting her to hurry with his meal. She bent to pet Cynthia, an orange-striped mother cat she'd found at her back door and Nubbins, a black tom missing one ear and part of his tail, nudged her hand, wanting a petting. "You're my family, aren't you?" Lacey whispered, uncertain as the painful memories enclosed her and tears began to flow down her cheeks. "You're safe with me and you'll always have enough to eat."

Gizmo began to bark wildly just as the front door crashed open. Birk Tallchief, wearing his western boots, and a big silky robe splashed with hot pink flowers stood in her doorway. A fiery wash of aspen leaves entered with him and the wind lifted his shoulder-length hair, gleaming black in the light. His steel gray eyes found her at once, locking onto her like a warlock who had sighted his prey. Lacey leaped to her feet when he entered her house, slammed the door behind him with enough force to rattle the windows, and walked straight for her. He crackled when he walked, a mixture of brown paper sack and plastic revealed beneath the silk robe. She wanted to laugh; she wanted to cry. Her safety, her defenses shattered like a brick wall slowly crumbling—

"It's time someone paddled your behind," he announced flatly, shoving up the big sleeves of the silky robe and jerking the sash tighter around his waist as he came to her. The robe flapped aside his long legs and Birk impatiently whipped the material around him. He scowled down at her, all enraged, simmering male dressed in a huge flowery silk robe. "One sock isn't enough in freezing weather, Lacey."

Lacey slashed her arm across her face. She wouldn't let him see her cry, ever. "It's your own fault. You shouldn't have kissed me in front of everyone. You've ruined my life. Now get out of my house—"

Birk bent down to look closely at her and Lacey hated the tear that lingered on her cheek and then dripped to her thermal shirt. Birk's scowl changed, softened and he grabbed her arm, tugging her closer to him. He leaned down to study her face and ran a thumb across her cheek. "You're crying."

She glared up at him; she didn't need his sympathy. She didn't need anyone. She could take care of herself. "Out. You have no idea what Gizmo can do to a silk robe. He's an attack dog, you know." She looked at Gizmo meaningfully, but the dog continued to noisily devour his bowl of doggie nuggets.

"I had to borrow this from Mamie Waters' clothesline," Birk stated ominously.

"You could have gone to Frannie's or to Doris's. They are miles closer to your famous sweat lodge. They drool when they know you're up there, hoarding yourself. You could have gone to Duncan and Sybil's—the Tallchief ranch is closer than Amen Flats. You had no right to kiss me like that...right in front of the whole town." She fed on her anger at him, let it devour her, anything but the pain lurking in her past.

His, "What's wrong, Lacey?" was too quiet, echoing softly in her anger, in her pain.

She pushed at his chest—pulled her hands back from the solid muscle beneath the paper and plastic, and eyed him. She didn't want him looking at her with those familiar, concerned eyes. "You stopped kissing my scraped knees a long time ago, Birk."

"Why are you really mad at me?" His hand brushed away a curl from her forehead, and stayed to scratch her head, a gesture he used to do when she was hurting as a child.

She wasn't a child anymore and she didn't want anyone's sympathy. Lacey lifted her chin; she had her pride, it had kept her going since she could remember. "Out," she repeated, dashing his hand away.

Birk studied her taut expression and braced his boots on her floor, crossing his arms over his chest and looking the long distance down at her. "You're hurting, Lacey. Want to tell me why?"

The question was too familiar, jarring her. "Those times are over, Birk. You can't make everything right now."

His black eyebrows lifted. "Can't I? Why don't you give me a chance?"

The child within Lacey told her to leap into his arms, to let him take care of her, just like all the Tallchiefs had always done. The woman in her told her that she could take care of her own business and that she didn't want Birk too close to her. The woman in her tangled mysteriously, just looking at him—all six foot three inches of ill-mannered cowboy, dressed in paper and plastic and Mamie's silk robe and his western boots. Maybe it was that part of Lacey that prodded her to tell Chelsey Lang that she and Birk had slept together—

Lacey scrubbed her palms against her thermal-clad thighs, wrapped her arms around herself and tapped her sock-covered toes on the rough flooring boards. She wasn't a child anymore and she wouldn't have Birk on a platter. "Eat dirt and stay out of my business."

She pushed back the curls that had clustered on her damp cheek. He'd ruined everything; he'd changed the way he kissed her. She'd needed comforting—her mother was coming back and—and Birk had changed the kiss, jerking away the underlying security she felt with him. Lacey rubbed her arms, feeling alone and vulnerable. There Birk stood, dressed in three-hundred-pound Mamie Waters's robe, and his boots and wearing a sock as a loincloth—yet he had never looked more like safety.

Lacey couldn't have him touch her; she'd cling to him and make a fool of herself. She was a grown woman now, not a child needing comfort— Lacey found herself running from Birk. She ducked under a line draped with her work clothes and drying over the woodstove. "Leave me alone!"

His hand flattened on the back door she had just reached, his body trapping hers. "You're in your long johns, Lacey. You can't ride that big Harley in your underwear and socks."

"Who are you to tell me anything?" She ducked under his arm, swung around a beam and threw the bra hanging from a nail at him.

That stopped him. Birk looked down at the flimsy white lace in his big dark hands and blinked. His thumb stroked the small satin cup. Then he carefully hung it back on the nail and shook his head. "Lacey, if you want to stop a man, you don't throw your bra at him."

All Lacey's nerves skittered to the top of her hot skin when Birk's smoky gray eyes prowled down her thermal-clad body. "You might try wearing one," he suggested unevenly as the sensitive tips of her breasts hardened.

"Who needs advice from a guy wearing a sock?" she demanded hotly and leaped to a big bag of dog food, then to the new stairs she'd just built. She had taken a few steps on her flight upstairs when Birk's hand wrapped around her ankle. Lacey jerked her leg and knew that he wouldn't let go. "All right, bubba, you asked for this."

She turned and leaped upon him; she'd always been faster and more agile than Birk and in another minute she'd be out the door—

Birk reeled back a few steps with the flying impact of her body, then his arms closed around her and he held her, her feet inches above the ground. "Do you want to tell me what this is all about?"

She attempted a kick and found herself lifted, carried like a child in Birk's arms to a sofa. He sat, trapped her legs with his, and held her wrists. Plastic and paper crackled beneath her bottom. "You know that I'm good at this," he stated. "Fiona wasn't sweet either when she got riled. I held you like this when you decided you didn't like me kissing Angie in the barn. You were only eleven then and you haven't grown all that much. I can sit here all night."

"So? You're bigger. You're stronger. And you were rolling in the hay with Angie. It's a wonder you didn't set the whole barn on fire the way you were kissing her." Lacey glared at him and fought the tears brimming to her lids. "Don't you have someone else to bother? Some bed you need hopping into?"

She didn't like his quiet, cool look. When the Tallchiefs got that look, nothing could stop them. Pauline Tallchief had that look the day she took Lacey's mother into a room and laid down the law. Jo MacCandliss's hands had shaken for hours later.

Lacey looked away from Birk's intent expression, her body trembling. Birk would get bored soon enough; he preferred holding tall, cool blondes with power curves. He shouldn't have kissed her with the Tallchief superkiss....

"Fine. Don't talk. You always were a pouter."

"Was not." She hadn't meant to speak to him. Lacey clamped her lips closed. Why did he have to know everything—almost everything about her?

"Were, too." Birk's tone held amusement and despite herself, Lacey turned to him. She managed a male work crew and she could manage Birk. "You shouldn't have mauled me at the wedding, hot lips."

"Hey, weddings get to me, okay? Elspeth is my first sister to get married. All those legends about the Fearghus dowry were coming true...first Duncan and the cradle, then Calum and the garnet ring and then Elspeth and the paisley shawl. I was emotionally delicate and you took advantage."

"Grow up, Tallchief." Lacey snorted delicately. "Me take advantage of the love-'em-and-leave-'em dating dynamo? Am I the last holdout against the great Birk Tallchief? What's the matter? Are you missing Chelsey Lang?"

Birk scowled down at her, his body tightening around her. "Leave Chelsey out of this."

"She dumped you, big boy. The second fiancée to dump the great Birk Tallchief in less than six years. Now, I wonder what made them change their minds...?" Lacey didn't want to think about the dark jealousy devouring her when Birk flirted with women. He enjoyed women, loved them, and she could have kicked him each time he drooled over another curved Amazon.

"By the way, your clothes are in your saddlebags and your horse was headed straight for Duncan's barn on Tallchief ranch. I tucked a note in, telling him not to worry. He's nice, so's Calum, but you're not." Lacey allowed herself a smirk; it was all she could do with Birk holding her wrists and trapping her legs.

Why was he smoothing her inner wrist with his thumb? Why was her pulse leaping to his touch? She watched Birk, the boy who had hauled her out from beneath the Tallchief house when she was hiding, brooding about her mother. He was the same and different—sage and sweetgrass scented his black glossy hair—and there were lines in his forehead and along his eyes—laugh lines, pale where the sun hadn't touched them. A vein throbbed in his temple and a muscle slid into his unrelenting jaw. He looked like his father, Matthew Tallchief, the kindest man Lacey had ever known.

Tense and wary, Lacey watched Birk scan her house, slowly, effectively hunting for something she did not want to share. Bred from hunters, Birk was the youngest of the brothers and potentially the most dangerous to her.

Because now Lacey knew that more lurked beneath Birk's charming exterior...he possessed the ability to tangle her emotions—

Birk had found the big dollhouse they had made together; she'd dreamed that one day they would share a home. She'd destroyed it when she was seventeen and hurting from Birk's rebuff of her attraction; then because it was a part of her life with the Tallchiefs, she'd rebuilt it. There were scraps of wallpaper from the Tallchief kitchen, a tiny rug from Elspeth's first loom, scraps of wood—

Birk looked down at her. "You kept it. I wondered."

Lacey didn't want Birk prowling through her softer emotions. Not now, not when her mother was coming back to Amen Flats and tearing away the safe world she had built. His gaze skimmed the airy, spartan, worn furnishings of her home and locked onto a framed photograph of the Tallchief family, given to her by his mother and sitting upon a woven length of Tallchief tartan. He glanced from the old iron bed in the shadows to the neat dresser to the pet baskets lining the wall nearby. His gaze lingered on Lacey's kilt hung neatly in plastic, and then moved to the drape separating the bathroom.

"That's right. There are no walls," Lacey stated impatiently as Dennis, a previous alley cat warrior, hopped up on her lap. His yellow eyes stared at the human male and he curled upon Lacey's stomach, stating his possession. Gizmo, at eighty pounds hopped up on the couch beside Birk and took in the situation with interest. Then he took a small blanket draped over the sofa back in his teeth and looked at Birk. Lacey closed her eyes. Birk would know—

"That's the old blanket, the one my mother made you, isn't it?" Birk asked gently and took the cloth from Gizmo. "You always had this wrapped around you, even when it was hot, when things were bad— What's wrong, Lacey?"

He'd released her hands and Lacey covered her face, trying to stop the sobs that welled out of her. Then he was just Birk Tallchief, who used to hold her when she cried and made her feel safe. Birk took her wrists and placed her arms around his neck; he placed the old blanket around her and over it his arms tightened around her. "Hold on, Lacey. Hold on and cry."

The gentle deep tone caused the pain to well out of her, and slowly, there in the house without walls and surrounded by her pets and covered with the old blanket, Lacey cried for the first time since she was seventeen. She knotted her fists in Mamie's silky robe, clung to the strength of Birk's familiar shoulders and cried, while he rocked her.

"She's coming back!" Lacey realized she'd sobbed against Birk's chest.

His finger tipped up her chin and he blotted her tears with the edge of her blanket. "Who's coming back, Lacey?"

"Ma." The word chilled her, frightened her. Not because of what Jo MacCandliss could do, but because of the painful old memories.

"You said she died, Lacey." Birk picked up a tissue and ordered, "Blow...now what's this all about?"

"You have to know everything, don't you?" she grumbled, trying to curl up into a small ball where the pain couldn't get her. "You always picked at everything then, digging out the facts. Everyone else thinks you're a charmer, out for fun, but I know you, Birk Tallchief. You dig and pry and lay everything in a neat row to suit you."

Birk only drew her closer to his hard, familiar body. "So that's what this is all about. Why you've got shadows under your eyes and why you—"

She scowled up at him. "I hit you because you kissed me like you'd kiss a woman you wanted, all right? The thought disgusts me."

Birk wasn't to be distracted. "Your mother is coming back and everyone will know that she isn't dead. They'll remember how it was, is that right? That she left when you were twenty and died in a bus wreck."

Lacey swiped her hand across her eyes. "Correction. She left when I was sixteen, and she'd been gone for weeks at a time before that. I didn't want anyone to know and—"

Birk's dark scowl frightened her. "So you stayed in that shack, forged the signatures you needed, and worked yourself to death. You could have moved in with us."

"The Tallchiefs were working hard to survive. You, Calum, and Duncan were working every rodeo possible to bring in prize money. You were going to school, running the ranch, and taking odd jobs to make more money. Elspeth was killing herself at her loom and minding the rest of you, and Fiona had a hard enough time just coping with being good and the youngest. I would have been just one more problem. It wasn't bad at all. Better than when Ma lived at the shack. I was warm in the winter. Thanks to Duncan and Calum and even you. I had plenty of wood. At least everything was clean, and I had plenty to eat—school lunches and working at Maddy's Hot Spot, cleaning up in the early mornings, there was always something to take home. I think Maddy saw to that. Once Ma's boyfriends got the idea to leave me alone—''

Birk inhaled sharply. ''What do you mean?'' he rapped out. ''Did they bother you?''

Lacey pressed her lips closed. She wasn't sharing anything more with Birk.

Birk glanced at the few clothes hung next to Lacey's bed and at the odd, used furniture and at the old power saw she was repairing on the floor. ''You didn't bid on that new contract—the addition to the school. For the last three years, you've been taking small remodeling jobs when you should have been taking bigger ones—''

Lacey yawned, exhausted by her raid on Birk and by sleepless nights. She settled down on Birk's comfortable lap and hugged Dennis close. ''So, who needs money?''

''You need a new power saw. Your whole company needs an overhaul. You need a new winter coat and coveralls.'' Birk stood, lifting her weight easily, and Lacey kept one arm around his shoulders. She wanted to push him away, and yet with the storms buffeting her, she needed his safety. She was too tired to fight, to worry about her mother. She buried her face in his warm, strong neck and let him carry her. She kept her blanket close to her; Birk wasn't much, but he was all she had right now. Lacey gave herself to sleep that had escaped her for three years.

Dressed in Mamie's silk robe and nothing else, Birk slid Lacey's bank statement and canceled checks back into the box. Lacey was right—he was good at laying facts in a row and building from them; he was also good at getting what he wanted. Her leather work gloves rested near her hard hat and both seemed so small and vulnerable. She'd been sending payments to her mother for three years and the sums had been growing. He added more wood to the stove, and looked to where Lacey lay curled in a small ball on her old iron bed. He rubbed his hand over his jaw, now covered with stubble. She'd left him with one sock for shorts and no clothes; he'd frozen his backside coming off the mountain and yet knew nothing could stop him from getting to Lacey.

He shook his head, stepped over Dennis, eased around Gizmo, who were sleeping on odd rugs, and switched off the elegant bordello chandelier, which Lacey had changed from kerosene to an electric fixture. In the dim light, Birk traced the open space and the electric wires. Lacey had done all this by herself, the blinds on the windows keeping her secrets.

She looked so small and vulnerable, lying under the bed's blankets. With a weary sigh, Birk grabbed a heavy folded quilt from a new shelf, shed Mamie's robe, hung it on a nail, and lay down beside her. He drew the quilt over him and placed his arms behind his head, staring at the new beams overhead.

He glanced at Lacey, the light catching on a shimmering tear, holding him. Birk moved slowly, cautiously, turning on his side. He hesitated a heartbeat and as Lacey shivered, Birk wrapped his arm around her and curled to her back.

He nuzzled the curls spiraling around his chin and let himself drift through the memories of holding Lacey on his lap, rocking her. He didn't know how, but he'd protect Lacey.

Gizmo leaped to the bed, sitting and showing his teeth at Birk. An odd assortment of cats followed, wading around Lacey and Birk to find a comfortable place. Gizmo issued a low growl and Birk glared back. Gizmo plopped down at Birk's back and pushed Birk closer to Lacey.

She sighed, curled her arms around the closest purring cat and scooted her bottom against Birk's lap. Birk groaned, Gizmo growled, cats purred and suddenly life seemed right.

Two

"What do you mean, you're at Lacey's house and you don't have any clothes? Your clothes came home in the saddlebags with a note from Lacey—what do you mean you don't have any clothes?" Duncan demanded, at seven o'clock the next morning. Over the telephone, his tone rose, wrapped in outrage. "Don't you know that she's never let a man in there?"

"She's half my size, her clothes don't fit me, and stop yelling," Birk returned as Gizmo took the edge of Mamie's robe and began pulling it. Birk held the robe with one hand, the telephone with the other and the assortment of cats twined around his bare legs. He jumped when a yellow cat licked his toe. He sat on the bed; Gizmo growled and showed his teeth. Birk jammed on his western boots and stood. "Just bring some of my clothes over here."

"You slept with sweet little Lacey MacCandliss," Duncan's statement was a low protective growl.

Birk must have slept a total of one hour and that was when Lacey chose to vacate her home—it was now seven o'clock in the morning and her hard hat and work boots were gone. Birk glanced at the rumpled side of the bed which Lacey had occupied...when she wasn't flopping over onto him. She moved restlessly all night, mumbling about mortar setting too quick, paying the mortgage and her mother needing a place to stay. Birk had found her leg between his thighs more than once. He knew exactly what soft part of her anatomy softly nudged his ribs when her arm flopped over him. She had rubbed her fingers across his chest as though he were a pet, and Gizmo had growled and showed his teeth at Birk.

And still, everything seemed to be right...as if she fitted into his life....

Birk shook his head while Duncan told him just how low he was. "Lacey? Lacey? Birk slept with Lacey?" Duncan's russet-haired wife, Sybil, asked in the background.

"You've got some explaining to do," Duncan stated tightly, and called away from the telephone, "Calum, Birk slept with Lacey—"

"Give me that," Calum said on the other end of the line.

"Me, first," Elspeth ordered in a tone that could lift the hair on the backs of the Tallchief brothers' necks.

"Does this have to be a family matter?" Birk grumbled as Elspeth took the telephone.

"Alek and I are here trading a ewe. I want more of the natural dark red wool for weaving. Calum and Talia came over with Kira—she's an angel, just like Lacey—but they're having some early mornings and came for coffee. That accounts for all of us. Just what do you mean by taking advantage of Lacey? She's more like a sister to us—"

In the background, Calum and Duncan issued growllike comments. Duncan muttered the words, "Bed-hopping Romeo."

"Hush," Sybil murmured. "Emily hasn't left for school yet."

"What's this about Birk hitting on Lacey?" sixteen-year-old Emily asked her mother.

"Explain yourself," Elspeth ordered Birk. There was no denying her imperial command, tossing Birk back twenty years to when he was fifteen, showing off and sniffing girls' perfumes.

"She took my clothes, Elspeth. Left me at the sweat lodge without anything but a towel and a sock—" Birk waited while Elspeth explained the embarrassing situation to the others. As he had with all of Lacey's escapades involving him, he braced himself for teasing. He scowled at Lacey's big dollhouse while a round of guffaws came from the line. He noticed a tear in the miniature roof, and crouched for a better look. Gizmo planted two big feet on Mamie's robe, defending his territory.

Birk traced the repaired fractures in the dollhouse. It had been demolished and carefully rebuilt. Lacey had lugged the dollhouse home when she was seventeen and her mother wouldn't have been around to wreck it. *He shouldn't have told her to grow up—that he couldn't babysit her all her life and that she should date boys her own age...there could be nothing between them—* Lacey's face had paled as if drained of blood, and then she'd punched him. He should have handled it better, but oh no, he had to sashay Loretta Miller in front of Lacey to prove his point. Maybe he did deserve the cold run down the mountain; maybe he deserved the Tallchiefs' dark storms.

"A defiler of women," Alek teased in the background. "Birk deserves what he gets. Don't take him the clothes. He can wear a sheet home. I'll see that the *Sentinel*'s photographer and a reporter covers the story—as the owner and part-time editor of the paper, I'll put the story on the front page. 'Tallchief in Toga' would be a great header."

"He's not getting Lacey," Duncan and Calum stated together and there was no laughter in their tones.

"No more baking from me, dear brother," Elspeth said in elegant, firm tones. "And no more hair cutting. You know she hasn't had a man in that house, and there you go playing games with her. Don't you dare hurt Lacey, Birk the rogue."

Birk traced a repaired inner wall on the dollhouse. He had hurt Lacey years ago, filled with the righteous decision that he was protecting her.

Forty-five minutes later, brick mortar plummeted down toward him, and Birk moved aside as it splattered on the muddy ground. The mortar plopped at his work boots, and Lacey scowled at him from the steeple of the church, three stories above. Wind caught the heavy, long ringlets of her hair, sweeping them from her long braid and lifting it wildly all around her face, like a witch's caught in a storm. Just looking at her dried his throat, the wind pasting her clothes against her taut body. Birk ached to wrap both hands in the whimsical soft length of her hair, and wipe her furious look at him away with a kiss that would remind her what could flow hot and urgent between them.

But oh, no, he'd handle her with patience and tempt her with his fine manners—until he could test what ran between them. Another glob of mortar plummeted toward him and he stepped aside, not taking his eyes from hers. He blew her a kiss and watched the fine fury rise in her cheeks, reddening them, the quick narrowing of her eyes, slashing down at him like fire skimming across the sky.

Birk admired the view, tantalized by the woman, enchanted by the excitement flowing between them. He'd made a mistake, choosing women far too tame, when Lacey's high moods caused his primitive instincts to rise. Birk narrowed his eyes. He might like primitive—with Lacey. The thought sent him reeling.

Jason Malone pushed a wheelbarrow filled with bricks past Birk. "Glad you're here. Takes the pressure off us. She's been too quiet and there's no chance of that with you around."

Jason, the best bricklayer in the state, had a soft spot for Lacey, and chose to work for her, despite Birk's offer. Lacey had taken Jason out for an ice-cream cone and told him that she was in danger of losing MacCandliss Remodeling if he didn't help her...though she knew that Birk's Tallchief Construction could offer him more money. She offered him a bonus at the end of the job and a discount on any building materials that remained. She tacked on free baby-sitting for two weekends while he and his wife were on mini-honeymoons.

Another sizable plop landed, splattering on Birk's boots. "Get away from my construction site, Tallchief," Lacey yelled, high above him. "Or can't you get any work? Jeez—do you work bankers' hours?"

Birk thought about the plans for the new school and the bid he was working on for a new wing—an emergency ward—for Amen Flats's small clinic. He thought about necessary overtime, the late lumber, the truckers' strike, and the bad weather coming. He watched Lacey ease along the high scaffolding, talk with another bricklayer, LeMont, and reach for a rope. Birk held his breath while Lacey placed her boot in a loop and shoved off with her other foot, swinging around to an empty window frame, which she entered in a neat, agile move.

Birk grabbed the church door, ready to— Then he saw Duncan's pickup pull up along the street. Calum's black sports utility vehicle parked behind Duncan's pickup, and Birk's two brothers leaned against the pickup frowning at him, their arms crossed over their chests.

"Elspeth wants to see you," Duncan the defender called. The name tags sprang from their childhood, when they were waving stick swords, and playing knights and damsels. Fiona and Elspeth sometimes had mutinied and played knights as well, rallying to a call. The play had served them well when they were working hard to stay a family. Lacey knew their names as well as Birk, and they had included her with "Lacey the lovely."

"Better cool off," Calum the cool added.

Birk inhaled sharply. All he needed was Fiona the fiery adding her two cents about how he should be nice to Lacey MacCandliss, who just then peered down at him. In her hand was another trowel sopping with mortar.

He sidestepped the mortar glob and blew Lacey a kiss.

"See you tonight, sweetheart," he called up to her. "Cook something, will you? I'll help with the dishes."

"Eat more toads!" she yelled back, the wind whipping at her clothing, her hair flying wild in the wind, escaping the braid.

Birk found the temper he wanted in Lacey, her blue eyes flashing down at him and her cheeks flushed with anger. He'd always been able to find out what was wrong in Lacey's life by revving her temper. With her mother coming back, something was very wrong.

Birk pushed away the memory of Lacey's mother clinging to him, offering her body to him. He pushed away her curses when he had refused her. He jerked on his leather work gloves and walked to his brothers. An inch shorter than his brothers and the youngest of the three, he'd always had to hold his own. "I'm going to Lacey's tonight, and if you want to sort that out right now, that's fine with me."

He waited for the solid impact of a fist on his jaw. Duncan looked at him coolly and Calum's lips remained closed. Then Calum said, "I hope you know what you're doing."

"I do," Birk returned and knew he meant it. He would protect Lacey from her past.

"She's fighting something, isn't she?" Duncan asked.

"You know that this could be a reckoning, don't you? That nothing has ever been easy between you and Lacey. Not since she was seventeen. She adored you until then."

Birk nodded and eased into his black, late model pickup—the custom interior victim of Lacey's skunks. Mamie Waters's round face peered through his windshield; she wasn't happy. "Lacey told me you stole my best silk robe, you pervert. You'll have to find an unmarried woman, because I am faithful to my husband. You're just a pretty boy, while Elmo is all man."

Birk handed her the silk robe and Mamie gathered it to her protectively. "I know that men want me...that my allure is fatal. But not one of them has stooped to steal my clothes. Shame on you, Birk. You're not a gentleman like your brothers. You're half my age."

"And he's unmarried," Duncan offered wryly, adding fuel to the fire.

"He'll have to find someone else. I'm taken." Mamie glared at Birk, swatted him with the robe and hurried off.

"Don't," Birk said as his brothers began to grin. "Just don't."

Lacey wearily eased off her motorcycle in the old garage and closed the doors. At eight o'clock she'd closed down the construction site, checked to see that plastic covered the windowless walls, and that all the equipment was properly cleaned and put away. She ached from head to toe, drained from a visit at the bank to extend an overdue payment, and a last look at her equipment told a sad tale. Broken-down machinery couldn't earn her a living. Birk was right; she did need a new backhoe to dig the sewer line, and a new power saw would be heaven. She'd have to ask Calum to sell off her retirement shares to add to her checking account.

She trudged through the dark and the wind, lowering her head against the leaves slashing at her. She took good care of her equipment—she wished she didn't have to work on that old power saw tonight, that she could just get to the end of the contract with it and the mortar mixer. Right now, all she wanted was a shower and a peanut butter and jelly sandwich—her usual fare unless she went to the café or to Maddy's Hot Spot. Then she'd work with the power saw, measure the plumbing pipe she needed to install in the upstairs bathroom, caulk the new windows against winter weather and put weather stripping around the doors.

If she worked hard and long enough, maybe she'd be able to forget that Birk had held her in his arms and the first of November, her mother's expected arrival date, was only two weeks away. Maybe Lacey would be able to sleep a few hours before the next work day began....

Gizmo lunged at her, playing around her legs and leaping against her. Lacey laughed outright. "Hey, I thought I left you in your pen. I'll bet you went over the top again, right? We'll have to change that—''

Gizmo growled at the shadows and planted himself protectively in front of Lacey, his hackles raised. She scanned the porch and seeing nothing, patted Gizmo on the head. Gizmo often showed off to passing rabbits and to the deer coming down from the mountain to water at night.

The first thing she'd do would be to change the sheets— she didn't want Birk's unique scent near her; she'd lived with it at Tallchief gatherings and when she was tormenting him. He would pay for tearing her secret out of her, pay for looking as if he wanted to fix everything for her—she could manage her own life! She caught a drift of his scent on the wind and shook her head. Lack of sleep and high emotions did strange things to the mind. She sniffed and decided that someone else's cooking had caught on the wind, sailing up to her home. Birk wouldn't come here again, not with the whole town laughing about him wearing Mamie's robe. Lacey smiled and walked up her steps. There was just something about tormenting Birk that made life right—

An old chair skidded across the porch and stopped, barring her from the front door. ''It's about time you got home, Lacey,'' Birk purred and strolled from the shadows to her, his hands in his back pockets. He'd showered, the scent of soap clinging to him, and the denim jacket, black T-shirt, and worn black jeans enhanced his bad-boy masculine look. The October wind lifted his shoulder-length hair and there wasn't anything kind in his expression.

''I see you've temporarily given up wearing women's clothes. Don't you have some work to do, Tallchief?'' She braced herself; she wasn't showing him her surprise that he'd come.

Why did she have to tell him about her mother? Lacey balled her fists. Birk had always known too much about her, sensed too much. All he'd ever had to do was to rev her up and she spilled everything to him—gave him what he wanted. She couldn't afford to give him pieces of her life now. She didn't want him too close to her, when she would have to fight to survive—

"I took the day off," he returned evenly, towering over her. "Come here." She opened her mouth to protest, then Birk tugged her into his arms and covered her lips with his.

Birk forced his lips away from Lacey's soft ones. He shouldn't have kissed her...shouldn't have held her tight against him and took her mouth as though he needed her to survive. He stepped back and ran his shaking hand down his jaw while Lacey stared at him, her lips still parted from his kiss. He'd barely stopped himself from slanting, deepening the kiss, but he wanted more than a kiss, he wanted some answers.

"There it is," he stated softly, watching her struggle for control while he wasn't certain about his. He'd been tracing her path up to the house, the weary slope of her shoulders, the slow plodding steps as if she couldn't drag herself up another one, and yet Lacey had survived— He hadn't meant to kiss her, but... "There it is," he repeated and knew that his attraction to her was stronger and more necessary than anything in his past...or perhaps his future.

Lacey shook herself, curls spiraling out to the wind, freed from her braid. Furious with him, her hands curled into fists. *"Get off my property."*

She pushed by him, jerked open the door, and walked into her home, immediately welcomed by her pets. Lacey paid no attention to them; she clicked on the light and faced him. Then slowly, slowly, Lacey turned to the stove and the soup Birk had cooked and to the bowl of fresh fruit on the old oak table. She scanned the neatly made bed, glanced at the stove filled with wood, and listened to the washer cycle and the dryer hum. Then Lacey turned slowly to Birk, who had just stepped inside her home and closed the door. She braced her legs wide and put her fists on her waist. "I don't need a houseboy, Tallchief."

"You were seventeen, Lacey. I was twenty-three and wiser." He shot that tidbit at her and let her gnaw on it.

"That's got nothing to do with anything," Lacey tossed back, sending him a slanted look. "Boy, you're low to bring that up."

Birk pushed down the storms brewing in him, the simmering need to take Lacey's mouth again. He needed to weed through her taunts and resolve this new facet to their ongoing battling relationship. "Why did you tell Chelsey Lang that I'd slept with you?"

"Because you did."

"Uh-huh. You were ten when my folks were murdered. You came to the ranch and wouldn't let anyone near you but me. Fiona was also in the bed and Calum slept on the floor. We had odd sleeping habits in those days, afraid that something would happen to the others while we slept. Elspeth and Duncan came in regularly to see that you were covered and warm. Elbows and knees kept me awake all night. I slept through math class the next day. I don't think that was the implication you gave Chel. And what was that about me being a 'walking sperm bank'?"

Chelsey hadn't noticed Birk reeling when she fed him that tidbit. But now Lacey saw that he wasn't up to playing her games. She was too tired to enjoy her victory and explained wearily, "That was sheer last minute inspiration. You're the only one of the Tallchief Black Knights who isn't taken. I told Chelsey that the Tallchief gene pool was prime, and that I was thinking about becoming a mother. If I couldn't get Duncan's or Calum's, I'd have to settle for yours before you got much older. I told her you'd probably populated a few households already and wouldn't it be nice if her future kids were related to mine."

Lacey tossed her hard hat to a table, ripped off her work gloves and plopped them in the hat. "Chel turned white. Imagine uptown, fancy Chel getting so mad over something so—innocent. You'd just won the motorcycle race and thought you had the world. You shouldn't have blown me that kiss—it's sure to bring results. It has always been my job to take you down a notch. I take it that the almost-engagement is really off—that the long, cool and stacked one has gotten away?''

Birk struggled to remain calm. He didn't understand what was happening to him. He understood why he needed to hold Lacey and protect her—he'd done that for years. But he didn't understand the undercurrents—his desire for Lacey MacCandliss. *When had she grown up?*

"The notches on my bedpost aren't that many, and none recently. I've begun to focus on the long-term. A relationship that will stand the weather." It was important that she understand something he didn't...why no woman had fitted him just right—until he'd held Lacey last night. Why he needed to feed upon her lips when she came home—why he needed to see her...to touch her...

Birk dismissed thoughts of Chelsey and her demands that he never talk to Lacey MacCandliss again. He tugged on Lacey's braid, loosened the band with a flick of his fingers, pushing the long black ringlets to those already free and wild. "You look like a ghost, Lacey. When was the last time you ate a real meal?''

"I pick them up at the other Tallchiefs' on a regular basis and they give me leftovers for keeping you on your toes." Lacey pivoted to Birk. "Don't you ever kiss me again, Tallchief. You're disgusting. You must have kissed every woman in town and most of them in surrounding towns.''

Lacey drew herself up to her full five-foot-three-inch height. The pride that had kept her going spread over her like a cloak, making her seem taller and stronger. He'd taught her that—giving herself the look of a bigger person to protect herself against the school yard bullies. "Don't ever...ever come into my home again. I don't need you.''

Birk hooked his thumbs in his belt. Just maybe he needed Lacey.

He studied her set jaw, the fire lashing at him from her blue eyes and the rigid stance of her curved body and the tight set of her lips. She was all woman and fire and pride, heat simmering beneath her freckles, in the flush moving up her cheeks. There wasn't much to her now—Birk realized that she could ill afford her recent weight loss.

He remembered her playing with the barn cats, riding on his back, and bent close to him as they had built the dollhouse. He'd seen every part of her life, the harsh reality of it, and for all those years, she was a part of his life, more like a sister than child who needed warmth and care. He saw her curled into a ball, crying beneath the porch, and he'd crawled in beside her, to hold her. She had the mark of the Tallchiefs, a tiny scar on her thumb. Yet somehow, she'd grown up. She was fierce now, as fierce as Fiona or Elspeth, when their moods were up.

Birk blinked. The child had become a woman. He blinked again and the memory of her body in the tight thermal underwear left nothing to his imagination. He could have put his two hands around her waist, but the neat flare of her hips ran into long, perfect legs. He thought of her breasts and realized how the upward tilt fascinated him, the two small tips intriguing. He shook his head and caught the fragrance of her hair, a blend of sawdust and sunlight and Lacey. He looked slowly down her agile body, dressed in dirty, torn coveralls and remembered how she looked last night in her thermal underwear, how she felt right in his arms. Birk shook his head again, dazed that Lacey fit him so perfectly after all the years of challenges and arguments and revenge antics.

The woman who fascinated him took two steps and hit his chest with her hands, the impact jolting him back. "That's it, isn't it? You're pitying me, trying to find a way to make it better? You thought you'd just come over and cook soup for me, do some laundry, and heat up the house and everything would be fine? That you'd give me one of those mind-blowing Tallchief kisses and everything would be better? Well, it isn't better, Tallchief. It's ugly and real and now, and if you tell anyone about—and that includes your brothers and sisters—about my mother deserting me, I'll never forgive you. I'm starting the rumor that she had an accident, amnesia, and all the while I thought she was dead. Chelsey was just a start, if you mess with me. You stay on your side of town and I'll stay on mine."

She seemed to grow as she spoke, a small fist grabbing his denim jacket, his undershirt, and a bit of chest hair. Birk winced and eased her hands away. She scowled up at him and prodded his chest with her finger to the beat of her words. "Now get this, Tallchief. I know you're emotional...I know it's October and what it means to you. You Tallchiefs get restless in October, because of your parents. I know you're...rather, your glands are missing Chel...I know that Una's legends are coming true—I've read her journals with the rest of you—and that you're dying to find the stacked blonde suiting you and have a houseful of kids. You've been working on the project for years, sifting through women. So...keep on working on it, and leave my life alone. When it comes to kissing, stick with women who find you interesting. Just because you're in need—of whatever—don't think that because I'm the only woman you haven't slept with, that I'm available. You're just plain unappealing to me, my prince," she added airily.

Birk absorbed the verbal slap and knew if he gave way to his temper, the war was on again. Gizmo showed his teeth and growled low, moving between Lacey and Birk. Birk stared at the dog and wanted—for some damn reason—to appeal to Lacey as a man. "Lay off," he ordered quietly and walked out the door with what little pride he could salvage.

Duncan jerked off his leather work gloves, slapped them down on the table at Maddy's Hot Spot. The manager of Tallchief Cattle Ranch eased into a chair opposite Birk and stretched his legs out in front of him. Birk ignored Duncan and continued studying the voluptuous nude painting on the wall. Duncan the defender wouldn't like Birk's thoughts concerning Lacey...about how he'd like to push the kiss further, to touch her tongue with his—it would be agile and sweet and— Birk glanced at Calum, who slid into another seat at the table. "You've got burp on your shoulder."

"Mother's milk," Calum corrected, unbothered by the fact. He lovingly smoothed two round stains on his chest where Talia must have hugged him; a nursing mother, Talia had been embarrassed more than once. One press of her breasts against anything, a strap, her husband, and milk surged out of her like a spring. Calum's enchantment with his wife had never been more obvious. "Mother and child are sleeping. That leaves me free to baby-sit you. She says you're emotional right now. That you've been acting pole-axed since you kissed Lacey at the wedding."

Birk snorted and hefted the mug of beer up to his lips. He set it down, flicked the price tag on the table's plastic roses and inhaled slowly. Maddy, the beefy bartender, pushed his well chewed, unlit cigar to the other side of his mouth, and slapped Birk on the shoulders. "Got it bad, huh, kid?"

Birk snorted again. He hated the fear in Lacey's eyes, and when she battled the past. She wasn't certain of herself, of how much more her mother could hurt her.

"It is October, Birk the rogue. You know how emotional and delicate we can be this month." Calum patted Birk on the back and grinned.

"Ah...have you been home yet, Birk the rogue?" Duncan asked, smothering a grin.

Birk dismissed his smirking brothers. Lacey's mother was returning; Lacey still loved her in a complicated way and Jo would go for that knowledge like a shark scenting blood. Lacey was unprotected, uncertain of herself, and aching from the past. Jo had been feeding on Lacey for years, now she was coming in for the kill, to suck away anything Lacey had managed to save.

"No, I haven't been home since this morning. I showered, checked on the construction and then took a few hours off." He'd parked on the street near the church and studied Lacey. Always an agile female, she took chances, and she knew how to order men, half cajoling them, with a pat on the back. But she'd learned well—a practiced eye checking the scaffolding, a small flat hand on the drying concrete, testing it for heat.

She'd started working on a nearby construction crew when she was just eighteen...when most girls were going off to college. Pop Ramirez said Lacey never turned down an order and she was the first one on the high beams, her workman's belt studded with equipment too heavy for her slight build.

"Birk hasn't been home yet," Duncan murmured and Calum lifted his brows.

"I had some things to do," Birk returned. Fed by the married members of his family, he rarely cooked. He hadn't realized that peeling carrots for vegetable beef soup took so long, or that thinking about Lacey and her kiss could make him forget the hours.

"You might want to go home now, and shovel the sand out of your kitchen. The MacCandliss Remodeling dump truck just happened to back up to your kitchen window and pour a load of sand through the open window—I have no idea how it got opened. Then there's the matter of the new brick wall covering your back door. The bricks are a great match, you can't tell where the door or the windows should be. The skunk odor coming from your house—if that's what you can call that old gas station—is enough to knock down an elephant."

"Figures." Birk closed his eyes, dismissing Mary Ann White's flirtatious ones from another table. He'd expected Lacey's revenge, for invading her fortress. At the grocery store earlier, LeMont had said that Lacey had taken an extra long lunch hour and had taken the dump truck, loaded with sand and bricks and mortar. Since Lacey frequently helped a family in need, her workers hadn't thought more about it.

Birk ran his finger down the cool perspiration of the beer mug and thought of Lacey's warm skin. Just then the rev of a big motorcycle curled into the tavern and Birk leaped to his feet, his pulses jumping at the thought of racing with Lacey, of running her down and—

He blinked again and realized that nothing excited him like chasing Lacey. He held absolutely still, enveloped by the thought of holding Lacey in his arms. He listened to his rapidly beating heart and to the hunter's senses within him.

Tallchief must have felt the same way when Una ran from him! Birk shivered, realizing that he was indeed emotional and fragile where Lacey was concerned. While his brothers and Elspeth were brooding over their heart mates, he had waltzed on with his life. Now, they were enjoying watching him.

Both Calum and Duncan shot out detaining hands, latching onto Birk's belt. "Whoa, Birk the rogue," Duncan murmured with a knowing grin.

"You really should try a gentler, systematic approach," Calum offered with a matching grin. "Flowers...presents...movies."

A woman eased closer, pausing near Birk. He ran his hand down his jaw and looked at the white, well-manicured fingers resting on his chest. He preferred another hand, smaller, with practical nails, one without layers of gold and diamonds. He smiled at Mary Ann, a woman who might have interested him before Lacey's kiss. But now, since he'd tasted Lacey, he wasn't available. He firmly eased Mary Ann's touch away from him. She lifted a casual brow and moved sensuously away. "Lacey says I'm unappealing," Birk brooded. "What do you know about that?" he mused, locked in the thought that Lacey could discard him so easily.

"You don't appeal at all to me," Maddy offered in passing, chewing on his unlit cigar. "But I wish you'd set up a regular time for coming to the Hot Spot. I'd get more women in then. You're the only Tallchief brother left unmarried. If the women are going to hunt you down, they might as well do it here, where I can make a profit."

There was only one woman who interested Birk at the moment—Lacey. He scowled at the revving motorcycle and knew where Lacey would go—back to the Mac-Candliss shack.

He didn't want her to face it alone. "I'll make myself appealing if it kills me," he muttered, striding out the door to his truck.

Three

_____

Birk climbed the ladder, propped against the old Mac-Candliss house, and sat beside Lacey on the rooftop. The owners, the Summers family, were away visiting, and in the moonlight, Lacey looked vulnerable, dressed in her black cycling leathers and boots, her arms around her knees. "Get lost," she murmured, her chin on her knees.

Birk didn't like feeling helpless and uncertain how to handle Lacey; her aching frustration brought back memories of the Tallchiefs trying to survive and the times when it looked like they wouldn't. But they always had each other. Birk withdrew his hand, just as he realized he'd been reaching to hold Lacey. She wouldn't appreciate the comfort, not now, with the past prowling through her.

"The least you can do is to let me spend the night at your place." One look at Lacey told him that she was riding a dangerous edge and apt to pit herself against anything.

For a moment, Birk turned the thought. He wanted Lacey to pit herself against him and in a changed way, more of a sensual, tender awakening—

She turned her head and slanted him a look. "Got you, didn't I? Don't you like wearing eau de skunk?"

"I've worn it before...the time you lured one into my car."

She shot him a wry look, the night wind drifting spiraled curls across her face. "The windows were so steamed, you wouldn't have noticed a forest fire around you."

He eased the curls away and noted that she did not move from his touch. He would be very careful with her.... "Let's go somewhere and talk, Lacey. This old roof could break at any time—"

"We've already talked too much, and the roof is good and sturdy. Shoring it up was one of my first projects, and shingling it with leftovers from Pops Ramirez's jobs." She suddenly placed her head on his shoulder as she did when she was younger and her world was rocky. "I stayed up here a lot when I was growing up."

Lacey turned suddenly to Birk, tears gleaming on her lashes. "I have no idea who my father is. She fed me that information early in life. Dad MacCandliss never liked her tricking him into marriage, and never liked me for living."

"Lacey—"

Moonlight danced on her lips as Lacey turned to him, her eyes mysterious in the dancing ringlets framing her face. "Duncan and Calum and Elspeth's legends about Una's dowry came true. Did you ever find the rocking chair?"

He skimmed back through time, remembering how she had cuddled on his lap, ten years old to his sixteen, and he'd told her about the legend. *The maiden who rocks upon the chair and sings a lullaby will claim the man of Fearghus blood who stands closest to her. She will be his heart and he will be her love.*

"I looked, and Sybil who runs down antiques and traces genealogy, worked on the project. It disappeared almost immediately after the sale to a pioneer family. The chair would be over two hundred years old and probably long past the termite stage."

"Really? Hmm. Then I guess you'll be a lonely old wolf all your life with no romantic legend to snare a woman." Lacey put her forehead on her knees, the small tight ball of her body causing Birk to ache. He reached to draw her against him, this new and familiar Lacey.

She slashed away his hand, but Birk turned his, capturing hers. She tugged her hand and he held tight. He'd waited all his life for her, the child-woman who made his blood leap with one look. Now it all made sense, why other women hadn't fitted just right—because Lacey had already taken his heart. He laced his fingers with hers and met her stare. "I'm in this one, like it or not."

In a heartbeat, Lacey jerked away her hand as if he'd burned her. "I'm going for a ride," she stated too coolly.

The hair on the back of Birk's neck lifted. He knew exactly where Lacey was riding, Murder Mountain, and the knowledge terrified him. He managed to snort disbelievingly and glance carelessly at her. "I knew you'd run from me."

"What do you mean?"

Birk formed his words carefully. "You're a coward, Lacey, afraid to talk with me. You're afraid to stand and fight, to stay anywhere near me and try to communicate on an adult level. You're hell bound because you realize that you made too much of that kiss at Elspeth's wedding, that you couldn't hold your own.... I cooked your supper. The least you could do is offer me something to eat and a bed for the night."

"I didn't eat your soup. I was afraid that you might have put something in it. I'm not your usual lady friend, Birk the rogue, and I only have one bed. As for stand and fight, you Tallchiefs taught me that and I have to see my mother again and face what happened to me. I'm not running away."

"Make that Birk the beloved. I'm going home—your home. I'll sleep on the couch," he tossed at her and watched her eyes light, focusing on him instead of the dangerous biking trail. He was moving into her life on a different level and he wanted her to notice the change. He eased to his feet and prayed Lacey would follow him. Minutes later, her motorcycle purred beside his truck and Birk pulled up the small knoll to Lil's Place.

What was he doing? The thought panicked him. He wanted to protect her, to hold her...but there was more. He'd never been stable where Lacey was concerned and she knew just how to unnerve him. He inhaled sharply when the moonlight caressed Lacey's leather-covered backside as she hurried up the stairs. She braced herself against the front door. "Exactly what do you want, Tallchief?"

He wanted to pick her up and kiss her. He wanted to wrap her in his arms and let that lithe body take away the pain humming through him. He wanted to tell her that the past would ease when once she faced her mother. He traced a fingertip down her hot cheek. "Let me in, Lacey."

He reached behind her to open the door and gently shoved her inside. The scent of her snared his senses. The hell with waiting. "Come here," he said softly, tugging her into his arms.

For a moment she was too rigid, her head back, blue eyes flashing at him. "What is it with you?"

Birk decided not to tell her; Lacey had always fought for what she wanted—he'd just have to make her want him. Instead he smoothed her hair and eased her head close to his shoulder—where it was meant to be. He eased her closer to his body and something within him gentled as if he were coming home. "I think we should get married," he whispered against the ear he wanted to nibble upon.

Lacey pushed back and stared blankly at him. "Tell me I didn't hear that."

"Okay." He gently pushed her away. He wanted to tell her more—he wanted to tell her that she was his friend and he wanted to be her lover, her husband. They knew everything about each other, and now he wanted to change the rules.

Birk inhaled and stripped away his denim jacket, carefully hanging it from a wall hook. He wanted her to get used to him living with her, loving her. He took off her leather jacket and placed it exactly next to his, then turned to her and pushed her down into a chair. For the moment, Lacey was shocked and malleable, and he knew his time was running out. Birk bent to unlace her boots, tug them from her feet. He rubbed them between his hands and studied Lacey's pale expression, her open mouth, and then lower to the tight sweater she wore. The hard lurch in his body told Birk that all of this was true, that he wanted Lacey for himself, to love, to protect. Before he kissed her, put his lips on her parted ones and told her too much, which would frighten her, Birk tugged off his western boots and strolled to the kitchen. He'd heated two bowls of soup and still Lacey hadn't moved. "Come eat, Lacey. You haven't touched anything. We'll eat and we'll talk, just like normal people."

"You've finally gone over the top," Lacey muttered as she slid into her chair at the table. She arched and rolled her body and a button gaped, revealing the smooth, firm line of her breast.

He'd seen her naked as a flat-chested girl, skinny-dipping with Fiona in Tallchief Lake. Now, he wondered, with his mouth drying, how neatly she'd fit into the shower with him. He remembered how agile she was and a sharp intimate jerk took his body to the aching level.

Birk shoved the bowl filled with hot soup closer to her and placed a soup spoon in her hand. He was angry with himself for the images of that tight, hot body curling around his; he was angry with her for not noticing him as a man. She would steam, smolder before he took her, and he would be her last lover. He half hated her for the need driving him, for the punishment his body would take before Lacey desired him. Oh, but she would desire him, Birk promised darkly, and he'd make her pay for every ache— "It's logical. I've thought about it all day and marriage to me would work."

"What? You've got a screw loose, Tallchief." Lacey crushed crackers into her bowl and stirred the mix. She began to eat hungrily, ignoring him. At least she wasn't throwing him out the door. Birk suspected that Lacey had no one to turn to, and that though she wouldn't admit it, she did not want to be alone.

Birk held a bit of cheese up to her lips, and without questioning him, Lacey took it in her lips. He wanted her to accept his proposal in the same way. "Marriages of convenience happen all the time today. The thing is to think of it as a business contract. You do your part and I do mine. Your mother will waltz in here, ready to…ready to do whatever she does with you, and she'll find you're a member of the Tallchief family. She'll have to deal with us…with me."

Birk knew just how he'd deal with Jo—hard and to the point—because she wasn't hurting Lacey again.

Lacey studied him with shadowed blue eyes, the color of clouds drifting over a clear mountain lake. "Why would you sacrifice your love life for me, Tallchief?"

Birk didn't intend to place his love life aside. He intended to begin one with Lacey alone. He reached to place a hot buttered biscuit into her teeth. She sat there, glaring at him with the biscuit locked in her teeth, and Birk knew that she wouldn't be easy.

You'll find a true love, Birk the rogue, but she won't be easy, his mother had said. *She'll be your match and you'll have no easy time convincing her that she's yours.*

Birk leaned back in his chair, studying this woman he wanted more than air. The black buttoned sweater and black jeans made her seem even more compact, smaller. He turned the thought; he'd always thought he'd fall for a tall woman, not one a good foot shorter than himself. But there it was, he decided, as butter dripped down Lacey's chin and he wiped it way with his thumb. Here he was, hot for Lacey MacCandliss and feeling tender and delicate about the claiming. On one hand he wanted to protect her from his desire, and on the other he was a bit more selfish….

Lacey ripped away the biscuit and chewed on the remainder, eyeing him warily. "I'm not marriage material, Birk-boy."

He shrugged and stroked the small scar on her thumb with his. "You're a part of us, Lacey. My family would make me pay if I didn't do something."

Lacey was up and striding back and forth, her herd of pets eagerly following her. Periodically she bent to pick up a cat and hug it, then began to pace again. With contempt, Birk knew that he was no better than her pets, wanting her attention. "I moved into your house today," he murmured, standing up and stretching as casually as if he'd mowed her yard.

Lacey pivoted, staring at him. "Birk, I'll have a crew at your house in the morning, cleaning it up. I'll go over there tonight and—"

"I'll help you tomorrow...when we bring over more of my things. We'll have to eat together at lunch and go out to Maddy's later, to show off our new arrangement. You'll have to hold hands with me, of course."

He wasn't giving her a chance to think, not now when he'd decided that she was the one he wanted. The loving would come easier to her, if he could manage his best manners and feed her a challenge a day. He rolled his shoulders and ripped off his sweater. Lacey had seen him work and play without his shirt, and Birk wanted her to get used to him as a man. At the slow, curious drift of her gaze down his body, he realized that his hands were shaking. He scraped the dishes, ran the water and began to wash them. Over his shoulder, he watched Lacey prowl through the airy house, followed by her herd. She noted his black briefcase in a corner, filled with his bids and estimates. She unzipped the bag he'd left on the stairs, filled with his clothes.

"Birk, one call to Duncan or Calum or Elspeth about my mother, and you're out of here."

Birk turned and flopped the dish towel over his shoulder, crossing his arms. "That wouldn't be wise, dear heart. Not once I tell them that your mother is coming back to roost. And then Sybil and Talia really don't like my brothers to

brawl and that's what it would be, if they tried to remove
me. I think Alek would understand perfectly. Think of marriage to me as an adventure, a challenge. Think how
shocked people will be. You like shocking people, don't
you?''

Lacey visibly paled; she bent to clutch an orange-striped
cat to her. ''I can't...I can't untangle it all,'' she whispered
and he knew she'd dropped into the past; Birk intended to
keep her attention on himself. ''A part of me still
loves...fantasizes what a mother should be, like your
mother was—warm, tender, spreading love around like it
was sunshine. Another part of me knows the truth and the
reality of what happened. I don't want children, don't know
that I'd be fit, because of her. I've been sending her money,
holding her at bay, because I knew one day that she would
come back and I wouldn't know how to—''

''I'll be right here, Lacey.'' Birk moved toward her,
watching her eyes fill with him. He took her hand and
placed it upon his chest. ''Right here.''

''Marriage has chains and lots of them.'' Lacey wrapped
her arms protectively around herself and shivered.

''You know it would work. You know that I wouldn't
mistreat you and that Tallchiefs do not—repeat, do not—
mess around while they are married. You'd be my one and
only love for the duration and we can dissolve it after your
mother leaves. You're a coward, Lacey, because it would
work and you need someone who can be with you all the
time. I'm that logical someone.'' Birk placed the taunt at
her feet and watched her temper flare.

''Who says?'' she snapped, her body taut.

He had her revving and deliberately pushed her again.
''You'll have to make me feel appealing...to make me
glow, if you want to pull this off. You'll have to act like
a woman and let me kiss you now and then—in public of
course. You'll have to touch me.''

He could have put more force into the punch that had
sent Billy Lord sprawling when he bragged about bedding
Lacey. He should have left Joe Phillips hanging from the

barn hoist all night for spouting off about Lacey looking "ripe for picking." But Joe had only taken two hours to convince.

"The hell I will." She glared at Birk, shouldered him aside and stripped on her way to her bed, leaving her clothes where they fell.

Birk traced her thermal-clad backside and the sway of her hips and followed her neat dive into the bed. "Don't let me detain you, honey," he called, nettled that Lacey didn't regard him as a potentially aroused and dangerously desirable male. Birk cursed silently; he'd find a way to make himself appealing and desirable. He watched the herd of cats leap up on the bed, the big dog following, and wished he were as welcome.

Lacey ripped off her hard hat and slung it on a pile of boards. She unstrapped the heavy belt she wore for lifting from her waist, and watched Birk ease around the scaffolding to her. He was twice her size and would probably eat most of the lunch in the picnic basket he carried.

She brushed sawdust and plaster from her cheek. She'd known him all her life. As a child, she'd loved him desperately. They'd brought Tallchief calves into the world and built a dollhouse together. He'd taught her how to rope and kissed her scraped knees when the calf ran, dragging her. He was a part of her life, twined in the bad parts and the good. The echo of his laughter was a part of her.

He shouldn't have kissed her at Elspeth's wedding…not a Tallchief mind-blowing, lip-sucking, heart-stopping kiss, drawing her up off her toes, seeking him.

He'd changed everything and she knew him for what he was…. Lacey pulled off her work gloves and flopped them aside as she sat on a board braced across sawhorses. She watched Birk leap over rubble, an agile big man wearing work clothes, his glossy black hair tossed by the wind.

There was no reason she wanted to smooth his hair, to feel the crisp texture against her fingers. His gray eyes locked on her and darkened immediately, as if she was exactly what he wanted. Lacey snorted. Birk was acting just like Duncan and Calum, moving in and playing the territorial male. When she was a child, they were her Black Knights, ready to rescue her with stick swords. Birk had come to rescue her once more. She shook her head and admired the width of his shoulders, the narrow hips and the long, long westerner legs down to his work boots. This morning she'd hurried to dress and found Birk sitting at the breakfast table, amid his paperwork. "Breakfast is ready," he'd murmured without looking up, and continued punching keys on his calculator.

He'd smelled wonderful, a soap and dark scent different from hers, and he'd shaved. The sight of his aftershave and razor on a shelf near hers had stopped her, the arrangement too intimate.

She hadn't slept in months, not a good refreshing sleep, and Birk sat in her kitchen as if he belonged there. "We've got to get the window insulation up this weekend," he had said, just as though he'd always lived there, blending with the seasons of her life. "Do I start a roast in the slow cooker for supper tonight, or are we going to the café?"

Her usual "eat dirt" return had seemed inappropriate, especially with Gizmo's jowls resting on Birk's thigh and Toto purring in his lap. Lacey decided she needed good hard work and thinking room, because Birk-in-the-morning was definitely too potent.

Now, only hours since he'd made his ridiculous proposal, he plopped the picnic basket onto her board, invading her life, and began to pilfer through the contents. The unique idea that someone was actually bringing her lunch had held her spellbound for one heartbeat. She'd just parted her lips to tell him that she didn't want him cooking her breakfast again and filling her coffee thermos and kissing her while they walked out to their pickups. Birk's brief, hard kiss stopped the tirade she had planned and then with an amused look at her, he sat on her board. "Miss me?"

Lacey munched on the tuna salad sandwich he handed her and eyed him. Birk blandly looked back, almost too innocent. She had a plan, built upon his, and somehow it all seemed right, but she hadn't worked out the details. His plan made sense. She knew she wasn't up to handling her mother, to dealing with the past—just thinking about it brought the ragged edges cutting into her. The Tallchiefs had always protected her. Birk, however, seemed to take a more than active interest in her. She tasted the drink he'd poured. "I should call the sheriff— What is this, milk?"

Birk bent to lick her upper lip. "Milk moustache. You need me, baby."

Lacey shook with the need to reach out and grab him, to hold him tight. "What are you doing?" she asked warily and knew that while one part of her trusted him—her almost brother—another part of her was uncertain. The uncertain part terrified her.

"Changing things," Birk murmured and leaned to kiss her again, this time more softly, a wooing of his lips against hers, a tantalizing brush of his mouth that swept slowly upward to her ear and lingered there.

The terror she'd concealed for years eased as Birk placed his face into the cove of her throat and shoulder. When he lifted his head, there was nothing brotherly in his gray eyes, rather a smoldering heat that caused her senses to leap....

"Don't touch me, Tallchief," Lacey ordered curtly at Maddy's. She couldn't think with Birk near her, his hand caressing her smaller one.

Birk's smoky gaze drifted lazily across her tight yellow sweater and his thumb smoothed the calluses on her palm before releasing her hand. He looked too big and too confident, used to playing games that Lacey hadn't played. He sprawled in his chair, dressed in a cream sweater that Elspeth had knitted him and western jeans and gleaming dress boots. He knew just what to say to make a woman glow, Lacey thought darkly. How to look at a woman and make her skin feel desirable...how to send ripples up a woman's spine with a touch on the back of her waist.

She wasn't used to light touches, protective touches from Birk Tallchief, as though he treasured her.

As if she was the only woman in the world for him.

He knew how to smell—that clean soap-and-male scent that drove a woman to desperation. Birk knew how to narrow his eyes and stare right into the heart of her, and start her senses humming. She needed to shock him, set his temper simmering, pull something that would— Lacey eased to her feet and then down into Birk's lap, placing her arm around his shoulder. She smirked at him.

Birk's expression darkened and there was no mistaking the firm wide span of his hand, riding low on her leather-covered hip.

Maddy, sashaying his beefy bulk to a table filled with tired, dusty wranglers, dropped the tray of drinks he was carrying. Milt Perkins's eyes widened and Eddy One Tree choked, spewing out the beer he had just sipped.

Lacey sat very still, aware of the hard thighs beneath her hips, aware of the tension that had suddenly leaped between them. Birk's voice was uneven and husky as he asked, "Playing games, Lacey? You have just told me not to touch you. So what are the rules?"

She ran a fingertip across his lips, intrigued by the firm, yet sensuous line. "There was a time between seventeen and twenty-one that I led a few boys on a merry chase. I've slowed down a bit and now only feed on one or two a year. I like to call the tune, not the other way around."

For an instant the fire she wanted was there, gleaming like hot steel through his lashes, then he snorted disbelievingly. "That's hard to believe. You kiss like a child."

"I've been around, Birk. You might be surprised. I could have steam hissing out your ears in two minutes." She had nettled him; he wasn't expecting her advance. "I always knew you couldn't hold your own."

Then because Birk had lifted one disbelieving eyebrow, she put her lips on his, parting them, to flick her tongue against his mouth. She drew back and grinned at his scowl. "Aye, you're a dark and brooding one after all," she murmured. "I've decided to marry you—temporarily, until you don't suit my needs. I'll think of you as a utility, and along the way I'd like to utilize your baby-making features."

The Tallchiefs had gotten to her, with babies tumbling everywhere, enticing her into motherhood. She wanted a baby, lying soft and warm against her, a part of her to go on, the best part. Lacey smiled, mocking herself. For all her independence, nature had come to call, beckoning her into midnight wake-up calls and the scent of baby powder. She wanted to give the world a small, perfect part of herself, the urge as basic as survival.

Birk's chest rose and fell unevenly against her. "Exactly what do you mean?" he asked, paling beneath his tan.

Good, she'd always liked to pounce when it came to Birk Tallchief—like the time he was skinny-dipping at the lake and she'd tied his clothes in knots and tossed them high in the pine trees. He deserved to be taken down; he had prowled through Amen Flats for years, wrapped in a power-male package that had women falling at his feet. "Since this is a temporary measure—and you'll be moving on, I'd like to change the business deal you offered. You'd be perfect and the only Tallchief available at the time. The Tallchiefs are genetically desirable. Basically, you're probably my last resource—I've tested all the rest in this town and they don't have those solid Tallchief genes. Other men want too much from me...you know, a commitment. But you're available now, and definitely not who I want to be committed to, so we could keep it light. You're the only candidate left, unless I choose artificial means, and that just seems so involved with legalities." Lacey wiggled her hips, so Birk would understand exactly what she did want. "Nothing too emotional, at just the right time for me to conceive. This would all be just as soon as my mother's visit is resolved, like a one-two plan, and then you can be on your way, no responsibilities."

Birk's surprised look changed to storms as Lacey continued, "Women have been chasing you for years, old boy. You've lathered up more women, had them drool, just by looking at you. Part of your desirability is that women want to bear your children—black haired, gray-eyed babies. You'll probably have a whole tribe of them with some overendowed blonde who you'll have so wrapped up that she won't know you for what you are. She—they can have you, right after I'm done with you. Wouldn't take more than fifteen minutes of your time, tops. You won't even have to pull off your boots."

She didn't trust his smile, or the icy steel of his eyes and the lock of his jaw.

"I see. You want to harvest me, is that it? No strings, no lasting affiliation—other than the one, a baby. We'd have to touch of course," he murmured too coolly, his hand caressing her hips. There was strength in his hand, possession as the hard, long fingers dug deeper into her softness.

Something leaped within Lacey, a tiny quiver of fear, quickly drowned by an avalanche of triumph and power. When she scored a hit on Birk Tallchief, rattled him, nothing was as thrilling. "Well. Barely. Just enough to get the job done. I know the mechanics and I'd sacrifice. Like I said, I figure about fifteen minutes tops, at the right time of the month. I'll take my temperature and time my cycle. I am going to resolve this thing with my mother and move on with my life. But there's no reason not to kill two birds with one stone, so to speak, while you're at my disposal."

Birk looked as if he were barely leashing his thoughts, and they weren't sweet. "I know that Tallchiefs love kids, Birk. You could visit and everything else, but you wouldn't have the responsibility. You could go on with your life without fear that you'd be paying—"

He took one slow, deep breath and hauled her to her feet. "Let's go."

Lacey blinked innocently up at him and smothered the laughter simmering inside her. "You're upset. Poor Birk."

Just then she saw that Tallchief steel, the hot look of his gray eyes, the locking of his body. "Got to you, didn't I, big guy?"

"Games, Lacey?" He showed his teeth and her heart

leaped, pulses humming. She had him revved, challenged, and nothing excited her more. "I'll think about it," he said too softly.

Lacey placed her hand along his cheek, the muscles tensing at her touch. She patted him lightly and watched his eyes narrow and flame. "Don't play with me, Birk. You're not up to it. If I want to run you down and bag you, I will. It's just that you're not up to my standards." She patted his cheek again, and felt the heat rise in him, the steam sizzle in the undercurrents. "Poor little Lacey has learned a few things, Birk, while you were out in the pasture, picking daisies and playing with the Nordic goddesses. I'm not a girl any longer, and if I wanted to make you sweat…really sweat, I could. There wouldn't be much left of you when you came up for air."

"You just could be overestimating your…talent, Lacey," Birk murmured and caught the third pat on his cheek, forcing her hand away from him.

Lacey hooked her fingers into his leather belt and tugged. "I've always been a bad girl, Birk. Especially where you're concerned. I've grown up. Maybe all those rumors about Racey Lacey are true. If I wanted to suck you dry, roll in bed with you until you'd flop around begging for mercy, take you and leave you brainless, I could. I've always been agile, you know. You're much slower than I am, and easier winded. You'd beg for mercy before I was done, Birk Tallchief."

"Shut up." There was nothing light in Birk's tone when he finally did speak. She watched, fascinated, as the storm brewed in his expression and his jaw locked into place. She batted her lashes and tilted her head, enjoying her win. Then Birk snagged her arm and dragged her out to his pickup. He ignored Maddy's friendly good-night, and Sara Jane's gaping mouth. While she was being dragged, Lacey licked her lips and smirked at Sara Jane, who had wanted Birk desperately since he was twelve. Lacey snuggled down in the passenger seat and reveled in Birk's grim, dark expression.

"Sara Jane stuffed her bra when she knew you were going to be around, and now she's turned to pure flab.... You drive like a sissy," she murmured as he slid through the gears smoothly.

Birk flung her a dark, impatient look and something hot and live curled around her. She pushed it away; she wouldn't let Birk start her skin dancing and her stomach churning. "I stopped worshiping you years ago," Lacey said quietly, meaning it.

"That's good. At least now I won't have to be careful with you, and ruin your good image of me," he returned and set the hair on the back of her neck rising.

Minutes later, Lacey grinned and hugged herself. Birk had dumped her in front of her house and raced off into the night, in a peal of his black monster's tires and changing gears. He wouldn't be making her breakfast in the morning, or spreading his papers on her kitchen table. She leaped onto her first porch step; she'd run him off, frightened him. She leaped to the second step; he'd probably pounce the first female he found and get engaged to her to escape Lacey. At least Birk wasn't looking at her with those concerned gray eyes, sorry for her. She didn't need his sympathy or his kindness, and cans of soup were good enough for her. She braced her legs apart on her porch and dusted her hands together. "That's that. I knew he couldn't take it."

Oh, she knew how to take care of herself when it came to Birk Tallchief. She'd always known how to rattle him. How to reach right in him and pluck a humming, too confident, masculine cord, just when he thought he had all bases covered. She wasn't what he wanted, what he expected when he tried tempting her like he'd tempted every other woman. Lacey knew him down to his boots and she wasn't drooling.

She licked her lips and smirked. She'd upset poor little delicate Birk, who had been spreading himself all over women for years. That was why he was just perfect for the child she wanted, because he wouldn't want to tangle with her, not as a woman.

Then why did the house look so empty without him? And why was she jealous, just thinking about Birk kissing another woman? Why did the past swallow her when he wasn't near?

Ridiculous, she thought, opening the old bordello door and stalking into the darkness of her house, immediately welcomed by her herd. She crouched to hug Gizmo and gather the nearest cat to her. She could beat Birk at any game he tried, and she didn't need his sympathy.

"It's for his own good," she whispered to Gizmo, rubbing her cheek on his fur. "Think of it...Lacey Mac-Candliss, who likes her life alone and simple, married to Birk Tallchief, the deluxe male on any woman's menu. He'll cool down and see that I don't need him anymore."

For just a moment, when Birk's body was taut beneath hers, Lacey feared that she could be like her mother—there were nice words for women who wanted men desperately and Lacey wasn't nice.

Lacey hugged Gizmo tighter. She didn't need Birk, not a bit. "That's all there is to that," she whispered to the airy space of her home, and her heart plummeted into a cold abyss.

Four

Birk fought his way through the feverish headache, surfaced, and found that he was sprawled in the middle of Lacey MacCandliss's bed. His throat felt as if it had been sandpapered and puttied, a headache throbbed within the brick wall in his head. He'd stayed away from Lacey for two days, licking his wounds, and a flu-stricken child's simple kiss had taken him down. He'd gone to Elspeth's with a nagging headache and Alek had taken one look at him, started brewing his wife's lemon tea for him and said firmly, "It's only the second week of October. We've only been married two weeks, Birk. You are not staying here. I'll call Duncan."

Duncan, fresh from building a fence, had arrived with Calum in tow and between them the three men decided that they didn't want him. "Lacey will take care of me," Birk had announced grandly, certain that the woman he adored would cool his fevered brow. He'd caught their evil smiles before they took him to Lacey's, propped him up, and pushed him at her. Because he was goony with fever, Birk had plastered her to the wall and placed his hot cheek against her cool one. Lacey MacCandliss was his oasis in the fever, soft and curvy and worried about him. "Save me, Lacey," he'd whispered, uncaring that the three other males were guffawing. "Your skunks have done a righteous good job at my house."

He held her tight, her curved compact body fitting his rangy one perfectly and tried to find her mouth. For just a moment in his fever, he felt her yield, a tender cool sweep of her hand across his cheek, and her blue eyes soft— "Oh, Birk." There was tender laughter in her tone; then she had squirmed and threatened and still he held her. The Tallchiefs had peeled him from her and despite her yells and threats, had carried him to her bed. He'd caught her wrist and dragged her along, until Calum pried her loose. "You shouldn't have done that, Calum the cool. She's mine. Dibs," Birk had groaned, swinging at his brother.

All night, Lacey had battered him with tablets and juice and menthol-laced salves beneath his nose; she plopped a thermometer in his mouth with as much tenderness as she would slap paint on a house. Her hand, rubbing menthol and eucalyptus salve on his bare chest, was an erotic caress to him. She had iced his aching head, muttering all the while.

He squinted painfully against the brilliant morning light as Lacey peered down at him. "I'm not happy about this, Birk, not one bit happy," she muttered and slapped a cold damp rag over his face. "You've kept me awake all night. This is what you get for asking nice little girls to marry you. I'm too good for you anyway."

He managed enough strength to drag the rag upward until it cooled his brow. Lacey shifted on the bed beside him, sitting cross-legged. "You should know better than to kiss a sick first-grader with the flu going around. Kids breed hardy germs. Great...little Mary Lou Banks skinned her knee while riding her bike, and there is the great Birk Tallchief, ready to kiss her bruises and make it better. But Mary

Lou had the flu, and it only took twenty-four hours to catch you, hot stuff, and make you weak as a baby. Open.''

She took the thermometer from his lips, glared at it impatiently, and shook her head. "Here the Tallchiefs came, with you draped between them like a landed whale. 'Alek doesn't want you exposing Elspeth to germs,' they said. 'Sybil is seven months pregnant, and Megan is just getting over the chicken pox, and Talia and Kira can't afford the flu. You did put skunks in his house.' There you were, draped between Duncan and Calum, and leering at me. 'Save me, Lacey,' you said.''

She shifted, the bed creaked and the church bell banging inside Birk's head slammed again. "I'm going to work, hot stuff. I'll come back in a couple of hours—all you'll do is sleep anyway, and your temperature is down. If you know what's good for you, you won't have a relapse. Sit up."

Lacey ignored his glare and pushed and shoved and maneuvered him until his head and shoulders were propped on the pillows. "Eat."

She reached over him, to pull up a pillow and Birk nuzzled her breasts, savored the scent and wallowed in the cool spill of her hair across his cheek. "I knew you'd be like this...big as a mountain and floored by a first-grader's kiss."

He snagged her wrist as she lifted the glass of orange juice to his lips. Lacey popped two tablets into his mouth and smirked while he tried manfully to shovel them down his sore throat. He wouldn't ask for her help, even as the tablets wedged in his dry throat. He glared at her, fighting the pain. She lifted her brows. "Thirsty, by chance?"

Birk released her wrist, drinking the cool orange juice greedily when she put it to his lips. "That's more like it. Now get this, hot stuff, you're a burden, you're not welcome, and if you let anything happen to you while you're in my care, I'll bury you in the next batch of fresh concrete."

He shot her his best deadly glare, weakened by the wet cloth sliding down his face. "You're cooler than last night and the flu only lasts a good two days, so I'm off to work. Here's the remote control for the television...a stack of builder's magazines...some computer ones.... There's the telephone. I'd appreciate it, if you didn't tell anyone you were in my bed. I never get colds or flu by the way, and don't appreciate having to take care of you. Don't expect my sympathy. Take the tablets, take the juice in the thermos, drink plenty of water and do not let any of your harem into my home."

She slapped another cold rag on his face. "I'll be home before noon, honey. Try to be a little sweeter by then. My, my. Such a look." She tapped his nose and smirked. "The whole town is talking about you dragging me out of Maddy's. They say that you've got a thing for me, and that you're acting just like the other Tallchiefs when you see the woman you want. But we both know that you'd never last, don't we? I've seen you in action, old buddy, with Emma Lowenski down at the creek, and you're not up to messing with me."

Birk glared at her as she pulled a sweatshirt over a tight T-shirt, and watched her swagger out the door in her hard hat and boots.

After the gong of her monologue in his head stopped, Birk promised himself she'd pay for that torture. Then the bed bounced and Gizmo leaped to his side, snarling. An infestation of cats followed, and a female leaped on the blanket over Birk's manhood, digging in her claws and purring.

The rest of the morning was spent in protecting his manhood, keeping his small wedge of the bed, and trying not to dream of Lacey's curved backside as she waltzed out the door. Birk snarled at Gizmo, and drifted back into sleep. Along the way, he decided he was just where he wanted to be.

Lacey stormed in at noon, before he could click off the soap opera he'd been watching. "Elspeth cooked soup," Lacey stated, pouring an aromatic liquid from a big thermos. She walked toward him, carrying a bowl and a dish towel. "You've gotten hairier than when you were in your twenties," she noted, spreading the dish towel on his chest.

"Go away," he managed through his aching throat.

"Yep, there you were, you and Emma making out while Cindy, Marge, and me took pictures—"

He shoved away the spoon approaching his lips. Lacey gripped a tissue and held his nose closed until he opened his mouth. She spooned in the soup. "It was a brand-new camera of one of Ma's boyfriends. Then Marge said you had to pay for having them developed, and none of us had money. But I still have the roll of film."

"My head hurts. Isn't there any mercy in you, Lacey?" he managed as she stuck another spoonful of chicken and noodles into his mouth. He closed his eyes, certain that Elspeth would heal him with the luscious herbs floating in the broth. Then he'd find more devious ways to get at Lacey.

"Nope. Not a drop of mercy in me. Not for you. Eat."

She peered at him and hooted. "I got you with the walking sperm bank, didn't I? Oh, the sheer joy of it. The great Birk Tallchief, wanted not for himself, his glorious loverboy reputation shot, but wanted rather for his genes."

Birk inhaled and decided that for now, Lacey's thigh beneath his hand was enough. The tip of her tongue appeared as she concentrated on feeding him, and he thought how marvelous she looked, pieces of sawdust clinging to her black ringlets, a spray of blue paint on her nose—only a shade lighter than her eyes—and a carpenter's flat pencil stuck over one ear. He wondered if she wore earrings and if she'd like his grandmother's pearl studs. He reached to rub the velvety texture of her lobe, to test the entriguing softness, and Lacey scowled back at him. "No touching."

He leered at her and licked her fingers when she brought the spoon to his mouth.

"I could dump this over your head," Lacey stated too quietly. "I could develop that film of you mashing Emma and sucking her mouth dry. But instead, I'll tell Sara Jane that you want to see her. She wouldn't mind the flu a bit, not if you gave it to her."

"Coward," he rasped through his sore throat. "I wouldn't mind sharing with you."

"I'm immune to you, Tallchief." Then she looked down to where Birk had laced his fingers with hers, drawing them to his lips for a kiss.

"When I return to the land of the living, we'll see about that. We'll see who makes who sweat and who makes who give, and who can lip-lock-suck who dry, shall we?"

She shot a sizzling stare at him. "Bubba, men don't live to talk when I get through with them. I'm small, fast and agile—they never know what hit them. I can fry brains with a single kiss.... That little challenge must have cost you pain. You sound like a bullfrog." She plopped a throat lozenge in his mouth. The fine tremor in her hand told him that she was affected, that he stirred the woman within Lacey MacCandliss. Whatever lovers she had, and Birk didn't want to think of how many or who, he would be the last.

In the afternoon, the telephone rang, Gizmo barked and cats looked lazily from their positions around Birk. Before he could rouse to answer it, Jo MacCandliss's husky tone curled into Lacey's answering machine. A man, clearly roused from sleep, muttered in the background. "Lacey, you didn't send enough money last time to keep me in beer. I need some new clothes and makeup. Send the check to the same address."

Birk slowly, firmly eased from the bed, disturbing the cats who then prowled around his feet as he moved purposefully to the answering machine. He erased Jo's message, grabbed the blanket that his mother had made Lacey, and eased his aching body back into bed. He stroked the blanket, drew it to his face and inhaled the delicate scent. *Lacey was his.*

Lacey dragged her hand across her face. She propped her stockinged feet on a chair, dug into the bowl of cold cereal—saving Elspeth's soup for Birk, because canned soup was all Lacey could manage to cook. She wished Birk wasn't within grabbing distance.

She glanced at him, sprawled over her bed, a tousled male lying in rumpled, rose-splattered sheets. The rosebuds across his backside did not shield the taut shape, and his tanned shoulders gleamed in the lamplight. He held her blanket as if he'd hold a woman, curved to him, his face nuzzling the well-washed flannel.

He'd frightened her throughout the night, the fever tearing at him. Lacey eased from her chair and made her way to Birk, followed by her herd. The angles of his face were harsh, jutting, masculine, a contrast to his long straight raven lashes. Stubble darkened his jaw and the pulse in his tanned throat beat slowly, heavily. She touched his rumpled hair, smoothed it and fought to tear her touch away. He'd showered during the day, not bothering to comb all that sleek, thick hair and it spiked out, tormenting her fingers.

She smoothed one warm, crisp strand lightly, then forced her fingers away. This was Birk, her childhood friend, who with his brothers and father had taught her that men could be gentle.

She shouldn't have told him about her mother returning to Amen Flats, because Birk had that Tallchief look as if they'd protect her through hell and back. *Why had she allowed Birk to enter her life, her home?* She'd stopped men from camping on her doorstep before, from getting to her, stopped them with one slicing word, a well-picked threat or a bucket of wet premixed cement.

She could marry Birk, just to make him miserable. He was right about that.

She'd fought him for years, pitted herself against him, committed to making his life an uneasy road. But nothing could thrill her so much as Birk on a rampage, yelling at her, threatening her, his temper like gunsmoke encircling him, sparks between them flying—

She reached to touch the spear of black hair on his forehead and Birk's gray eyes opened to look at her blankly.

The look held, changed to heat, smoldering and igniting the sparks within her. The next instant he tugged her into bed and before she caught her breath, he was sleeping again, his sigh deep and sweeping across her cheek. "I've always hated you," she whispered to the night as Birk nuzzled her hair. "You're arrogant, high-handed and macho. You swagger, think you're God's gift to women, and—"

"You'll marry me." Birk's deep voice stroked her ear, chilling her instantly. "Just think of it, Lacey. You'll scoop me away from all those willing softhearted women. You can make my life hell—day and night. You could be even more inventive, having me around all the time."

She shoved free of him, surged up the stairway, and picked up her hammer, pounding away at the flooring. When she couldn't pound another nail, her arm feeling like lead, Lacey switched hands and pounded more. When she couldn't continue, she put down the hammer and tried not to think about the wild emotions Birk created in her.

She glanced at the old rocker; it seemed to glow, the rich wood warming as she looked closer at it. She sensed other women, in another time, treasuring the chair and soothing the babies in their arms, creating peace and harmony, and making the world beautiful. She was a woman, yet she had experienced little of the tender emotions. How would it feel to have children, nourish them, and keep them safe? She wondered, drawn to the old chair. How would it feel to sing to them and hold them and know that they were safe in her arms? Then she took the old rag doll from the small rocker in the shadows, held it upon her lap and began to sing a lullaby that Pauline Tallchief had sung to her. She looked out at the stars in the night, gathered the old rag doll closer and rocked as she softly sang nursery songs.

The shadows stirred and Birk, dressed only in a towel, sat on a sawhorse. He smiled coldly and crossed his arms over his chest. A tiny vein pulsed in his temple. "Finished hammering the living hell out of my skull, darling?"

Darling. The word curled around her, winded her and left her mindless. With Birk's reputation, he probably used it with every woman. "I was making music. I've always wanted to be a drummer," she lied while her heart flopped and leaped and tumbled. No man had a right to be that sexy, a long angular line of muscles and cords and covered with gorgeous tanned skin. The scar running across one shoulder and down his taut stomach glinted in the dim light, reminding her that he'd run down the calf she'd roped. He'd pitted himself against the young bull and eased the rope enough to untangle Lacey. Then he'd kissed her and cuddled her and told her a story about elves to make her laugh. "Elf," he'd called her back then.

The moonlight shafted into the darkness and Birk found the old rocker, testing it with a prod of his foot. Lacey held her breath as it rocked slowly. "Unusual design. Light, handcrafted—"

She had to distract him; the rocker was hers, purchased from an old man's truck—sold to buy his cemetery plot. She couldn't let Birk know that she'd had it for years, hoarded it. She'd wanted a legend to keep her safe, like the Tallchiefs had claimed theirs. *The maiden who rocks upon the chair and sings a lullaby will claim the man of Fearghus blood who stands closest to her. She will be his heart and he will be her love.*

Birk's big hand was smoothing the thick varnish over the tiny carved flowers at the top, tracing them intently. He restored furniture beautifully, but rarely kept the pieces for himself. He'd helped Sybil clean away varnish to find trademarks, and when he wasn't tracking or crafting a Native American canoe from a solid log, or panels of birch bark, Birk was a master at old furniture. She could see the slow recognition in his expression, the concentration—she had to distract him.

"You'll have to say yes, because I won't ask you," she hurled at him, fearing he would discover that the rocker was likely to be Una's. Sitting on Pauline Tallchief's lap, Lacey had seen the drawing in Una's journals and had recognized it at once. She'd captured Una's rocker to hold the Tallchiefs close to her, some bit of their lives, their heritage, that she could cling to and imagine that she had had a family just like theirs. "You say yes, and we'll put the walking sperm bank idea on hold."

He frowned, his hand roaming on the black layers of varnish, seeking. "Yes?" he repeated absently.

"I won't ask you, and I don't want to say yes to anything you ask, so if you say yes, we can try that convenient marriage. Just until I deal with my mother...I have to do it by myself, work it out. You've got to promise you won't make my decisions for me, Birk...that you won't take matters into your hands. I'm tired now, and probably not thinking straight." She ran a shaking hand through her hair, mopping it away from her face. "I'm definitely not thinking straight, or I wouldn't be considering this...game with you. I'm not a little girl anymore and I wouldn't like you interfering between me and my mother. I know that I have to work this out, but it is nice to have you nearby—rather like a big yard dog, if the going gets too rough. And you should know that I hate admitting that."

"No more pounding hammers?" he asked with a smile that captured her heart.

When had things changed? When hadn't their lives blended? She could trust him to stand by her and with the past tugging at her feet like deadly quicksand, she needed him close.

Birk gripped the chair in one hand and found her in the shadows. Moonlight glinted in his eyes, silvery steel locked on her as he worked his way through the agreement between them. He gripped the back of the rocker as though it were his right, as though she were his in the bargain. "We'll have to spend time in the Bridal Tepee. It's a Tallchief custom I don't want to break. And I don't want my family worrying about me...or you...so we'd have to kiss. You might have to sit on my lap—and stay if things get warm between us. You'd have to promise me a bed at night—I can't go running to my brothers and sister when you toss me out."

Lacey squeezed the doll, an old one of Fiona's, rescued

when Fiona would have tossed it away. "Deal. You won't, of course, drool over anyone else during the contract. You'd be on a diet, and no more tall, cool, stacked ones in tight, slobbery clinches. And you've got to promise not to interfere with my mother. And you have to realize that I'm very much better at winning what I want than you are. When it comes to your love life, all those plush jobs with running heaters wouldn't be on your diet. That's the beauty of this—you without your harem."

"We'll see." He eyed her from head to toe and back again, slowly, and taking in her thermal underwear. "You might want to buy some lighter gear, something in silk and lace. This could get sweaty."

"And wet," she tossed at him, to keep ahead of the game. "You haven't said yes yet."

He reeled with her last taunt and Lacey allowed herself a long, slow stretch, arching her body and yawning. She found what she wanted in Birk's expression. "You're drooling for me, darling," she whispered. "This should be interesting. By the way, I wrote down all the women's names you called out in your fever. I intend to blackmail you, when I can give it my full effort. Maybe I'll hire a big plane that will write across the sky, "Birk loves Stella and Nancy and Joan and—"

He lifted his brow and placed his hand against her cheek. "Jealous?"

"Of course not," Lacey lied and holding his eyes, turned her lips to kiss his palm.

He took the challenge and patted her cheek before removing his hand. While Birk looked at her, he touched the old rocker with his foot and the old bordello settled around them, creaking with age and the slight wind battering leaves against the window. "I should have handled you differently when you were seventeen. I'm sorry I hurt you."

Lacey leaped to her feet, hurrying down the stairs, away from her shame when she first admitted she loved him. She grabbed her blanket on the way to the couch and waited while Birk settled into bed. The silence stretched into minutes and Lacey didn't move.

"Yes," Birk agreed finally in a husky, deep tone that rattled her nerves.

She tensed. "Yes?"

"To marrying you. There are certain traditions to be observed. I'd like to be married on the mountain, where Una grazed her sheep and where my parents are buried. I want my family to be there."

"That would be nice," she whispered and shivered. She needed all of the Tallchiefs around her; it seemed right.

"So, here we are," Lacey murmured as Birk carried her into the Bridal Tepee. The third week of October, the wind howled down Tallchief Mountain, whipped the pines, stirred the leaves, and topped the black lake with white crests.

Birk placed her on her feet, stood back and looked down at her. He seemed to see inside her, to all the little edges and raw places, ready to bleed. Lacey swallowed and held her breath as Birk's long, slow look took in her beaded doeskin shift and her feet, encased in beaded moccasins. The shift was old and revered, worn by other brides. Lacey's small body had required thongs around her waist, wrapping the shift to her and the fringes moved seductively along her arms and legs. Birk's hands cradled her cheeks, and she gripped his wrists. He was her anchor against fear, as he had always been.

"You are perfect, Lacey," he said.

"It's just like you to say something like that now. Why couldn't you stick to—?" she began as the tear burned its way over her lid and down her cheek.

"Because you are." He spoke in the same firm tone as when he took his vows in the wind-kissed knoll up on the mountain. The Tallchiefs were buried nearby, and with the growing Tallchief family and friends nearby, the day didn't seem so cold, only the terror in Lacey's heart. She'd sur-

vived the teasing, the bridal preparations in the prepared
tent, the toasts and Birk's tender kiss, sealing his vows.

Another tear slipped down her cheek. He shouldn't have
kissed her as if he'd give her all the days of his life, all the
sunshine in his heart, and never fail her. He shouldn't have
tasted of kept promises and tomorrows. He shouldn't have
kept her close as if nothing could take her away, as if he'd
be with her forever. He shouldn't have fitted the picture of
a groom candidate, but he did, looking at Lacey with those
smoky gray eyes, touching her gently as October swirled
around Tallchief Mountain. He towered above her now, her
new husband, her old friend, and tormentor. There was
nothing sweet about him—

Birk's thumb brushed away her tear and took it to his
lips. He touched the tiny rosebuds in her hair, smoothed
away the ringlets from her brow, holding them back as he
studied her face. "You're beautiful, Mrs. Tallchief," he
whispered reverently, thrilling her, frightening her.

"Oh, hell," she muttered, the tears welling out of her.

His smile was teasing, gentle. "You wouldn't get emotional on me, would you, Lacey?"

Good old Birk; she could count on him to save her. "Not
a bit. How long does this tent gig take?"

"Two days. I'll start a fire and see to Storm Maker."

Lacey plummeted into the uncertain bog of what does a
new bride do while awaiting the groom. She looked around
the tent, laden with herb bundles and cooking gear and the
big down-filled sleeping bag. She'd brought jeans and
sweatshirts and thermal underwear, not sexy nighties. *She
must have camped with the Tallchiefs a hundred times, and
yet—*

Birk grinned, gently taunting her. "You're going to help
me take care of my horse, aren't you? What kind of a
woman lets a groom freeze his rear end on their wedding
night?"

Lacey released the breath she'd been holding, tossed the
fears away as Birk tugged her out into the freezing night
air. Tallchief Lake tossed white waves into the night, the

pines whispered, and Lacey dived into the fresh, clean scents, aware that Birk held her hand, had gently wrapped his arms around her, bringing her back to him. "Your tush is safe with me. This is not so bad," she murmured as the wind whipped her hair and Birk's long hard body warmed her back. She leaned against him, glad for the warmth and the old friendship. "Not bad at all."

Birk bent to murmur in her ear, his lips just touching her. "You wouldn't try anything tonight, Lacey, would you? I'll bet that if I hold still, you can't make me tingle…not one little toe-tingle."

Lacey smiled in the cold night air, promised herself that she could make him tingle, and sweat, and— She turned slowly to him, this man she had married, still dressed in traditional buckskin and fringes, a long-legged Westerner, just begging to be taken down.

Lacey stroked the fringes on his chest, traced the blue beaded designs crossing the width. She peered up at him and traced her fingertip across his lips. Just looking at Birk heated her, the temptation to make him steam better than he had ever steamed before, ruling her. She tossed away caution on her quest to take Birk Tallchief down. "I'm better than television. You might not be able to take the pressure."

He snorted in disbelief, taunting her. Yet his fingers soothed her nape, a caress she didn't trust.

"Who says?"

"Look at me, hot stuff. Do you really think you can take the heat?" Lacey licked her lips, placed her hands on his shoulders and stood on tiptoe to kiss his cold lips. She brushed her mouth across his, catching his scent, diving into it.

Birk sighed as though bored. "Storm Maker is waiting. My gelding isn't used to being decked out in flowers and herbs."

"Elspeth, Sybil and Talia insisted on decorating your horse. So did Duncan, Calum and Alek. And by the way, Tallchief, I prefer to ride my own horse, not to ride in front of you, sharing a saddle with you. No one told you to wrap me in your mother's hand-stitched quilt and cart me off before the party was over." She jabbed his chest and when Birk shoved away her hand, Lacey's temper ignited.

She followed him to the horse, carefully capturing the flowers and herbs that he tossed her way, hoarding her wedding day. "You're evil-hearted, Birk. Your family worked hard to—"

He hefted the saddle from Storm Maker and eased the gelding into a shelter covered with branches. Lacey gathered the cold bouquet to her and hurriedly followed his long strides to the immense wood pile. "Who cut all that wood?"

"I did. Stop pestering me."

"Birk, that's enough for all winter and then some."

"So? I was restless."

Lacey tested the unweathered end of a wood chunk. "It's all freshly cut. You cut wood when you're upset. It's an odd therapy, but you used to do it when you're really—"

Birk glared at her over his shoulder and continued loading wood. "You won't pester me all night, will you? You haven't said a word all day. You've been pale and cold and shaking for most of it, as if you were being led to death row...and now— Suddenly when I like quiet and being alone, you start pestering me."

"Oh, I'll pester you all right," Lacey promised, following Birk into the tepee. She hoarded her flowers against her while he built the fire. Not a single herb bundle or flower was getting away from her, neither was one Birk Tallchief.

Birk prepared dinner, trout fresh from the lake's weir, baked potatoes, and a skillet of cornbread baked in the coals...and Lacey never gave him a moment of peace, asking questions that she knew the answers to, and while he was simmering, she studied her captive and planned how to torture him more.

The firelight spread on his harsh angular features and Lacey traced Birk's Sioux heritage, and his light gray eyes, a gift from his Scots great-great-grandmother. There was a tiny scar on his cheek, the one he'd gotten trying to shave when fuzz first appeared. There were the fierce angles of the hunter, the black glossy hair no longer sleek, but tossed by wind and the impatient stroke of his fingers. Lacey smothered a smirk; she was getting to him, slowly and very effectively.

She scanned his broad shoulders, covered now in a familiar worn flannel, and the length of his worn denim jeans down to his moccasins. His long tanned fingers were too capable, too steady, as he shoved her plate to her, ignoring her. He was all hers—a personal challenge.

The wonderful nugget on the balancing scale was that she trusted Birk on a level that she trusted no one else. "Birk, you are typically Tallchief. You wear the Tallchief pride and honor like a badge. Nothing could make you break a promise, once you gave it. But I truly believe that if you didn't use caveman strength—okay, I admit you're stronger and bigger—that I could make you steam. Is that all you can do, is snort?" she asked, her temper rising, challenged by Birk.

He stood abruptly, sweeping away the dishes. "I'm going outside."

"Fine. I'm going to bed, honey." Lacey blew him a kiss and smirked again when Birk scowled at her. She slowly unwound the thongs from her waist, and lifted the bridal shift from her, leaving her in her thermal underwear. She held his eyes as she stretched and bent to unlace her moccasins. There was interest there, mild, but male interest, laced with humor.

"Figures," he murmured. "Thermal underwear on a wedding night. Most real women would have chosen lace to interest a groom. Not that I am interested, because this is a temporary measure, remember? Then I'll be out there sampling the juicy stock—"

That ignited her, made her want to ruin him. Because she knew that she was ultimately safe with Birk and because his lifted brow mocked her, Lacey swept down her thermal leggings, shimmied out of them and braced her hands on her waist. Birk glanced mildly at her white cotton panties; his cool look at the peaks of her breasts caused her to heat. Then he left the tepee.

Lacey dived into the giant sleeping bag, shivering as the cold cloth hit her skin. She promised what she'd do to Birk if he came near her—either hit him in a vulnerable place or—

Lacey awoke to Birk's warm body lying next to hers. The wind circled the mountain, swished the trees and she was awake immediately. Birk's arms were folded behind his head and he was studying the smoke-hole in the center of the tepee. He turned his head to her in a rapid movement that hunters use when sensing they are being stalked. They looked at each other, his gaze stroking her face as if he'd remember it forever. He frightened her now, though she knew his Tallchief honor and pride would keep her safe.

"You're taking up too much room, Tallchief." She started the volley.

Birk grunted and flipped to his side, giving her a view of his broad back. Lacey frowned; he couldn't ignore her. She surveyed the wide expanse of skin, found a perfect gleaming spot and kissed it lightly. Birk jerked instantly, flipping around to her. "What are you doing?"

She loved his outrage. She'd scored a hit. Lacey placed her hands on his chest, stroked the hair growing there, pushed her fingertips through it, and reveled in his textures, his scents. "I've gotten to you, haven't I? You wouldn't be able to lie still if I touched you, would you?"

Birk did not move as her hand lightly skimmed his face, his shoulders— He didn't move as she eased her bare leg closer to his and then pushed away in surprise as her body lurched. "Birk, you are naked. Here with me."

"Shocked?" His smile was so devastatingly male delight and evil, she wanted to wipe it from his face.

Her body ached, her breasts in particular. She flopped away from him and then back. "I know. I'm not generous in the breast department."

"I said you were perfect. I meant it."

"That's just like you, saying things you don't know about. I want you to put your hand on me, Birk and tell me that I am, even though I'm half the size of your preferred stacked and cool ones."

"Lacey," Birk warned, and she knew that she couldn't rest until his hand touched her breast. She sat up, jerked off her thermal shirt and let him study her breasts in the firelight. Then she shimmied down beside him, holding the sleeping bag up to her neck. "What was that supposed to prove?" Birk asked, in just the right outraged tone she thought she wanted.

"No one seemed surprised when we said we were getting married," she wailed after a full moment of debating what troubled her. His tone had set her off balance and nothing was going as she expected. "They all seemed to be expecting it. This is no good, no good at all. Here my mother is coming and I can't even steam you enough to make the whole thing look real—"

Lacey sat up, her hand on his chest. "I'm not afraid of her, Birk. Don't say that I am. But...but," she floundered, drifting back into the childhood she remembered, still clinging to the smallest kindness her mother had given her...a prescribed kiss, a required hug for an audience. "It's all tangled up," Lacey admitted, feeling as if she were very old and drained. "Part of me loves her, and part of me is afraid, because it isn't logical."

Birk stroked her hair, the way he'd done when she was little. "It will work out, Lacey."

"It's rough," she stated shakily, begrudging the admission.

"I know. But you've always handled it well."

"Yeah, right. Here I am, an idiot for getting into this marriage thing with you—"

Birk's fleeting look of pain stopped her from going on. The Tallchiefs took marriage seriously and though he was only standing by her through a rough spot, she shouldn't have hurt him. He was only acting honorable as Tallchief men do when protecting those dear to them. She knew she was dear to Birk and to the rest of the family; he was only acting as he thought he should. The storms were hers, frightening her and she shouldn't take it out on him. She kissed him quickly, to mend the infraction. Because she needed to distract him and herself, Lacey flipped over onto Birk. "Lay still, Tallchief. Hold still, and let me terrify you."

Lacey stretched out on him, held his jaw between her hands and kissed Birk with every bit of skill she could manage.

Five

Lacey was only experimenting, Birk managed to think as his body jolted into fierce need and her open, soft wet lips moved upon his too hungrily. She was using him as a distraction for what troubled her, and despite his honor, his body didn't object. Her bare legs were long and smooth against him, her thighs slender and strong.

Her hands moved upon his shoulders, smoothing them, and the tiny calluses were familiar, an erotic, unique roughness compared to other women's softer hands. "That's right, keep your hands from the rest of me," he managed, dying to have her touch him.

Lacey eased to straddle him, to brace her hands on his chest. The firelight played across her face, her shoulders, caressing the tops of her breasts and— Birk dragged in air as Lacey's plain white cotton panties rocked gently over him, the heat of her dragging every vessel in him to an alert mode.

"You're so easy." She grinned and dived down for a kiss that left him stunned.

"Who did you vamp in those busy years between seventeen and twenty-one, and who were the one or two a year after that?" Birk heard himself say. He'd kill them for teaching her this, how to devastate him, make his body leap against his will...for touching her and taking what little innocence her mother had left her.

"You Tallchiefs can be a scary lot, protecting us defenseless women. There they were, the three Black Knights, ready to kill the first boy I dated. But they weren't boys, Birk the rogue, they were men—"

Birk found his hands on her thighs, a possessive gesture, as he tried valiantly to keep his eyes above her shoulders. "I should have killed Ted Gilquist."

"You almost did." Lacey smirked, and took his hands, lacing her fingers with his as she pressed them down beside his head. "Tell me you're fascinated. Tell me you haven't been trying to ignore the fact that I have compact, but efficient breasts."

She glanced down, hesitated and before Birk could move, Lacey bent to suckle his nipple. "Lacey!" He wished he hadn't sounded so outraged and old-fashioned. He wished every molecule in him didn't want to—

Lacey's tongue was just as agile as her body, entering his lips and teasing him. "Hold me," she whispered in an aching tone. "Put your arms around me and hold me."

Birk forced himself not to concentrate on the breasts lodged firmly against him, dragging the hard little nipples across his skin as she moved. "This isn't how it's going to be, baby," he whispered, firmly removing her from his body.

He planned to seduce her, to take her in a way that would erase all other men.

"I could take you in a minute tops," she flipped back, crossing her arms across her chest and lying too straight and tense beside him.

Birk lifted her palm to his mouth and flicked his tongue over the center. Lacey tensed even more and Birk allowed himself a long slow look down her body. "I'm old-fashioned. I go for protocol. You could kiss me."

She shook her head. "Oh, no. You'll try to make me moan and groan—"

"And purr," he corrected, blowing the curls by her ear. "And simmer."

"Bull—" Lacey held her breath as Birk eased over her. "You are big," she whispered unevenly. "I mean...I always knew you were, so are your brothers, and Elspeth and Fiona are tall. But you—you're winding me, Birk. There's too much of you, close up."

"Scared?" Birk eased his weight gently down upon her. She'd known other men, but he wanted to let her taste his weight, the feel of him against her, because he was surely the one who would have her last....

Her lips tasted warm, seductively innocent against his.

"I've never been scared of you, Tallchief."

"That's good, Mrs. Tallchief." He underlined his possession, a small concession to the pain gripping his body. He reveled in the tension humming through her body, in the restless shift of her hips, the sucking in of her stomach. "Just how much do you know about what I want?"

"I know the mechanics. I've been here before."

Birk raised higher, facing her, and not shielding his fury. He didn't want to think of the men that had taken Lacey. "Not with me, you haven't."

Her fingertip strolled down his tense cheek. "Hey, I offered."

"You were seventeen, Lacey," he stated after a flat curse.

"And ripe. I wanted you, Birk. I wanted you desperately and you turned me away. I had to take alternative measures to feed my wicked appetites."

He'd hurt her and could never forget the shimmering blue of her eyes, like an icy film clouding a clear fresh summer lake. "That's because I always knew that eventually, you'd come asking me to marry you, Lacey Tallchief."

"I never asked. You gave yourself to me on a platter," she whispered back, her lips just touching his. She wrapped her arms around his neck, and toyed with his hair and studied him. "You're flushed and feverish, Tallchief, and I don't think it's a reoccurrence of the flu. What's that? Steam coming out of your ears?"

"You'll have to heat me up a bit more before I'm interested, Lacey, and in the meanwhile you'll be purring for me, begging me."

"Is that so?" Lacey tugged his head down, her tongue shot into his ear, jolting him. "You're slow, Birk."

"Am I?" His hands eased from her small waist, up her ribs and his thumbs smoothed the outsides of her breasts.

"Do it," she ground out, shaking under him, her heat and excitement steaming beneath his hands.

"Mmm?" He continued to stroke her soft skin, easing his hands to fully capture her. Her body tossed against him and Lacey closed her eyes, shaking. "I won't hurt you, Lacey."

"I know. It's just that...I hadn't expected to be so involved...."

Birk caught the back of her head, bringing her lips to his and nibbling upon them. "I intend for you to be very involved. You can't just jump on me and have me, because I'm not an easy game. You'll have to work to get me." He kissed her with the heat within him, not shielding her from his desire. When her lips were hungry for his and her body flowing into his, bumping him rhythmically as the sounds came deep from her throat, Birk eased her away. She shook and he knew why, yet he wanted there to be more to the lovemaking than the mechanics. He wanted more from Lacey Tallchief than her body.

He stroked and caressed and whispered to her, bringing her back to the Lacey who could trust him, then he gathered her into his arms and held her tight as she drifted into sleep.

She made him pay the next day, carelessly dressing in front of him, and Birk knew that at any moment she'd attack him. Lacey jerked up her jeans, as he studied the perfect shape of her breasts. "Oh, Lacey..." Birk swept out an arm, catching her behind the knees and bringing her down to wrestle with him.

"Get off me, you over-sized—"

He kissed her then, the light kiss of friends about to become lovers.

She eyed him and he waited for the thought scurrying around in her brain to come out to scare him. "Birk...would you take a sleeping woman? I mean that seems so—"

"Why, baby?" he asked, the tenderness he felt causing a warm glow.

"I ache this morning, Tallchief, for no reason. My...my...upper story hurts and I feel like I could chew through a pine tree and run through a brick wall. I'd like to tear you apart and—"

He kissed her again, a light peck of understanding. Whatever, whomever she'd had, she hadn't stayed long enough to understand the depth of a long, satisfying lovemaking event. "Your 'upper story' is perfect. Maybe this will help," he offered and lowered his mouth to her breasts.

Years ago, when she was budding, she'd told him they hurt, and he'd sent her to his sisters. She gasped as Birk flicked his tongue across the sensitive peaks, blowing on them until they were hard. Then gently, so gently he brought her to his mouth and suckled tenderly. "There's this, baby," he whispered as she shivered and grasped his shoulders, her fingers digging in as he wanted.

He ran his hand down her curves, smoothed her stomach and went rock hard as she quivered. He kissed her breasts softly as he slid his fingers beneath her panties and lower—

Lacey went still, breathing hard, waiting for him, her pulse quickening.

Birk forced himself to move slowly, to trace her femininity as her damp heat poured onto him. Lacey's hips bolted upward at the first rippling constriction and still he held her beneath his touch, smoothing, caressing, suckling at her breasts, taking the hard pebbles deeper.

She rocked against his touch, bolted again, surprising him, and wilted beautifully while he fought the need to take her. Her eyes were soft then, tender upon him, weighted by her fulfillment. Then she pushed him away, scrambled to her feet and Birk knew that an elephant couldn't make him move, he hurt too badly. Lacey dressed furiously, pausing only to throw whatever she could find at him. "Dirty, rotten, low-down playing, Birk. How low can you get?"

"You're not aching now, are you, baby?" He grinned, certain that a quick dip in the lake would cure his ache, but he intended to have a more satisfactory curing from Lacey...when she was ready.

She made him pay. The new Mrs. Tallchief made certain that she sat on his lap whenever possible, that she kissed him until he ached for more, and curled against him—when they were in public. In the two days since they'd returned, Birk hadn't stopped aching. He took long, slow and cold showers.

Everything seemed gloriously normal, with the exception of Lacey's mother's visit next week and Lacey sleeping on the couch.

Lacey was back at work, striding along the high rafters, dancing along the scaffolding, and cursing the weather, a mix of drizzle and autumn, changing into winter.

At eight o'clock in the evening, Birk inhaled the aroma of the roast in the oven, and settled down to work on the old rocking chair. He knew what lay beneath the layers of old black varnish and began slathering on a mixture to soften them. With the cold wind whipping the old bordello, bringing the rocker back to life seemed appropriate. While Lacey had made concessions to the downstairs, and he'd moved in his share of furniture with the help of his brothers, the upstairs had a spacious, raw glory all of its own. There were no walls, just mounds of new wood, pipe and rolls of insulation. The windows were sound and Lil's favorite colored-glass window gleamed in the rigged light hanging overhead. Lacey was working late, pushing to meet her contract and she'd come dragging home at any minute.

Birk smiled; just to look at her filled him. He would pick her up and snag a kiss before she caught her breath, and peel her clothes from her and plop her into the new bathtub with the claw feet. He grinned and ran a small trowel over the curved slat, scraping away layers of black goo. He'd always been good with his hands and he intended to give Lacey a home, filled with— The rose he'd expected yielded to a Celtic design and down on the runners were marks— *Fearghus*, it read, when he pushed through the indentations with a pencil.

Birk sat back, winded. Written with care and love, Una's journals had perfectly described the small rocking chair with Celtic markings across the back. *The maiden who rocks upon the chair and sings a lullaby will claim the man of Fearghus blood who stands closest to her. She will be his heart and he will be her love.*

Lacey was no maiden; she'd made that clear enough. Birk frowned, and scraped away more layers. Fine, he wasn't a virgin, either, so they were on equal terms. He worked quickly stripping the softened varnish away from the cherry wood—wishing he'd known she'd been alone, that her mother had deserted her...wishing he'd been gentler with her at seventeen. He swiped the sweat from his eyes with the back of his hand and used a toothbrush to clean the small Celtic designs.

He had what he wanted, the chair and the woman. All he needed was time to tame her, to seduce and slide her slowly into the long-term marriage he wanted. Birk smiled, pleased with himself, and caressed the smooth wood that had emerged after a scrubbing with linseed oil and turpentine and brush of fine sandpaper. Tallchief had sold cradles to pay for his growing family, and Birk knew where one could be purchased. He could be quite persuasive when he put his mind to getting what he wanted, and he wanted Lacey.

Lacey crouched by his side, startling him. The scent of her, mixed with wood and concrete and sweat, eased the wild mood riding him. Her thumb ran over the Celtic design at the back rail and drifted down a slat. "I wondered. It's Una's, isn't it? A piece of her dowry, sold to keep Tallchief land."

"She tamed him, the chieftain who had captured her," Birk murmured and brushed sawdust from her hair. He touched the scratch on her cheek and wished he could heal the scars of the past.

"After your parents were killed you held me on your lap. You told me how you had a plan, the five of you, for staying safe. How you planned to take back what was yours, the Fearghus dowry, sold to keep Tallchief land. How you had each raised your thumbs to the storm and just when the moon shone like a silver disk, you all shouted, 'Aye!'" Lacey ran a lazy fingertip over the old wood, loved by another woman in another time. "I knew it when I saw it, knew that this lovely old thing was what you sought...and knew that I'd never let you have it."

She hooked her thumbs in her jeans and tilted her head. "That's the price for the kiss-off when I was seventeen, dear Birk-boy."

Because she was challenging him, taking him through the pain and back into a time when his heart leaped at the sight of her and his body craved what she offered, Birk stole a kiss. "But I've got you now, don't I?"

Lacey sent him a look. "It's a question of who has who, Birk the rogue. You're not out there sipping every flower, now are you? Your Tallchief pride wouldn't let you go running to the arms of other women, would it? You're my captive, so to speak. The opportunity to make you miserable was too good to pass. Your supply has been cut off, Birkie-boy."

Birk allowed his gaze to stroll over the cocky, feminine supply he intended to keep, to cherish for a lifetime. Her jeans were torn at the knee—Lacey's jeans were always torn at the knee and worn too thin. She should have been taking care of her needs, rather than supporting her mother's vices. Birk fought the temper riding him. "You've been giving your mother money for years."

Her blue eyes shot to his and she shrugged. "She needed it. I didn't. You don't understand about her, Birk, so don't make judgments. She gave me what she knew to give. Her life was worse than mine, by far."

"That makes it right, does it?" Birk stood, wiped his hands with a rag and wanted to shake Lacey.

She was on her feet, ready to fight him. "You had a family, and a good one. It makes a difference, even Una's legends kept you safe. You had something to protect you. My mother survived the best she could."

Birk remembered how Jo survived with a bottle, boyfriends and neglecting Lacey. He shot out his hand, cupping her chin. "Don't tell me you excuse how she treated you."

She dashed away his hand and stalked down the stairs, her bootsteps echoing like shots. He wouldn't be discarded and found her stripping near the bed, tossing clothes furiously to the floor. "I see you've moved in, taking all the room with your old furniture."

"You've got plenty of room, Lacey."

She scanned the wall, found where he had hung Tallchief's musket and powder horn, crossed with a big broadax. Slowly Lacey looked to where Birk had placed a huge antique, humpbacked chest, layered with his buckskin shirt and pants. Her gaze dipped to the long flat wooden bowl and the assortment of primitive knives which Tallchief had used for fashioning the cradles and hewing Una's bread bowl and spoons. Beside the long bowl were a stack of smaller bowls and a basket decorated with colored porcupine quills. Inside were spoons designed for children's hands, the shafts layered with the Tallchief Mountain symbol and the stick man and woman figures.

Lacey took out one of the small spoons, smoothing it in her hand. "Elspeth said that Una wouldn't have her children eating with their fingers."

She found their Tallchief tartans and kilts, hung side by

side, as he wanted their lives to be. She whirled to face him, her face pale with fear. "Birk, this all looks so permanent...your things mixed with mine. I thought we could keep this on a light—"

"Catch." Birk tossed a small package to her. His night of romance wasn't starting well.

"I'm tired and I'm in no mood for games—" Lacey ripped open the package and hesitated. Her fingers picked at the leather fringes, and touched the Native American beading—the Tallchiefs' mountain symbol and the stick man and woman on the flat leather bag. "This comes from Tallchief."

"Aye," Birk answered huskily, wanting to snag Lacey in his arms. "It's for my bride. Open it."

Lacey carefully eased open the bag and five huge perfect quartz crystals tumbled into her open hand, catching the light. "What are they?"

"Because he had no jewels or wealth to give her, Tallchief gave Una a crystal for each child she gave him. I know where the cave is on Tallchief Mountain, and she probably never knew how dangerous it was for Tallchief to get her gifts."

Lacey moved her hand and the crystals caught the light, sending a myriad of colors across her face. She carefully eased the crystals back into the bag. "I remember. Una's journals, portraying their love, seemed like a fairy tale to me. It still does..."

Lacey studied Birk. "You look like your dad. Like Duncan, Calum, Elspeth and Fiona. Black hair, gray eyes, steady, good people who love their families, and treasure children. You can't hold me on your lap anymore, Birk. You can't put my head on your shoulder, and tell me elf stories and those of Tallchief and Una."

"I'm Birk, darling, the same as I've always been." And different, he thought, tossing in a bit of honest grit. His desire was no small element in his emotions concerning his wife.

"Do you think I'm like my mother, Birk? Do you?"

Lacey demanded. "That's part of the reason I want to see her again. Because I have to know what's in me and what I'm made of. I have to untangle the knots to go on."

"You're a part of us, Lacey the lovely." He used the Tallchiefs' endearment for her.

She glared up at him. "This is too easy, Birk. And you're not an easy man. You've always been a handful, playing jokes and laughing, and teasing women until they drooled. Now, here you are, moved in with me, cooking and cleaning, and—and it's all too easy. It's too easy to know that you'll be here when she comes. That you'll understand the past and what it does to me. I don't like it a bit."

She stalked the length of the old bordello, her hands in fists. Then she turned to him. "You're so confident of who you are. So arrogant, standing there, big as a mountain and zapping every woman who comes near you. I wanted to teach you a lesson."

He braced himself for the storm brewing in her, and decided to be patient. Then Lacey gripped his shirt, and a bit of chest hair, and her lips were too close to his. "You're mine, Tallchief. I ran you down and bagged you."

Birk traded his patience for his hunger and pride, snaring her close. "Are you certain you're the one who did the bagging?"

That sent her head back, eyes flashing. He admired the proud set of her jaw, the fire broiling him, washing against him. "There will be no women for me, Lacey," he vowed, meaning it.

"Oh, I know. Your family would stake you to an anthill, if you hurt me, and how I'd cry, Birk...you'd be surprised how injured I can look—mmm!"

"Threats just excite me, darling. Why don't you take a bath and cool off," he whispered when he was finished kissing her. Birk eased her slowly to the floor and walked to the kitchen area, where he could vent his frustration on vegetables. He'd had all he could take of Lacey at the moment, without taking the game—his intimate needs, he corrected—further. So he gave himself to the carrots, peeling and chopping, and to the potatoes, tossing them in with the roast. He found himself sniffing past the cooking scents, to the ones coming from behind the curtain, the ones curling from the old-fashioned bathtub and his wife.

Just past the bathroom drape, a dainty, foam-laced foot braced on the curved edge of the tub. Birk's instincts told him to join her, it would be easy enough to let lust take him quickly. Birk inhaled the tantalizing scents and decided that he'd let Lacey call the shots and come to him. She'd always been stubborn, picking her own way through minefields, and if he pressed her too much, too soon, Lacey would get her back up and he'd have to start all over again.

This was what he was good at, crafting plans to take on solid form. Though they had skirmishes, they were friends already, linked to the past, and to his family. He was just changing the structure, rearranging the bricks and the boards to last.

Birk washed his hands over his face, in an effort to replace woman scents with onion, and found Lacey, dressed in his chambray shirt, running for the table by the door. "They came!"

"Mort Williams caught me at the post office and asked me to bring them for you." Birk watched, fascinated as Lacey ripped away the brown paper from the biggest box, from a mail-order catalog, too light to hold winter clothing. She laughed and twirled, holding a scarlet teddy decked in black lace close to her. She held up a rainbow of silky bras and stringlike panties, and tossed another scrap of a negligee over the couch.

Lacey tore into another package, the heavy one, and squealed with delight. "Oh, I couldn't afford it, but I just had to—the *Kama Sutra*. With it, the mail-order catalog was having a special, offered overnight delivery, and I had to order the whole Ultimate Lovemaking Collection of books. A perfect how-to for women. It occured to me that I've missed a few fine points in my education. There was a time when I wasn't interested in sex, but now I see that I'm behind, and it's time to catch up."

She held up a racy black lace outfit to her, swished it in front of her, and eyed him. "When I was seventeen, you put a severe dent in my love life and I leaped into men without taking time to savor them, or to have them appreciate me. I've decided that there are finer techniques, like finishing concrete properly."

She swirled a scrap of panties around her finger. "So here we are. Married. Just you and me in an old bordello, which almost moans with the sex, and you betting me that you won't beg. We'll see, won't we, Birk the rogue?"

Birk couldn't move, his eyes blurring with images of Lacey dressed in the sexy lingerie and stalking him. In his hands, the dish towel ripped.

Lacey almost felt sorry for Birk Tallchief, because she intended to teach him a lesson. She had scored a hit, and Birk was sulking, taking one of those long showers that kept her from nettling him. She stood by the beautiful old tub, admiring it, and brooded about the crystals. Birk had no right to give something so precious to her, as if she were really his wife. She glanced at the circular curtain, sealing him from her. "I like the tub," she called, over the sound of running water. "How much do I owe you for it?"

"Get lost." Birk's muffled reply set her off.

"You can't hole up in there forever, you know, sweetie. Tonight, I'm going to study my erotica collection and practice moaning. You'll be able to hear me from the bed. You can give me tips on panting."

Birk jerked aside the curtain and peered out, scowling at her, his hair slicked down to his head, water dripping from his sharply etched features. For a moment, he frightened her, and she knew what Una felt when she had tested Tallchief to his limits. Then when Birk ripped the curtain closed, Lacey decided shakily that he was just Birk, the same as she'd always known.

Lacey scooped the ringing telephone from the cradle, and heard her mother's voice. "Why haven't you sent the money? Here I am, stranded in Seattle, no clothes and no makeup, nothing but what I managed to take with me in a bag.''

Jo's husky voice had lost its sexy wrapper and was now demanding, the hard voice Lacey remembered. ''Hello, Mother.''

''Who would know it, the way you treat me. I'll be there the first of November, in just a week, and you'd better have a nice bed for me. I'll need a heavy coat for Wyoming—I always hated it there. There's no place to shop and I'll need things. You'll send money, won't you, Lacey-honey?'' Jo asked in a softer tone that caught Lacey. ''You've never failed me, honey. Not when I really needed you.''

Lacey glanced at Birk, standing beside her, a towel wrapped around his hips. She wasn't ready to tell her mother that she'd married Birk, and hated herself for being a coward. Birk crossed his arms over his chest and stared at her with eyes as cold as ice on steel.

While her mother itemized her needs, Lacey sensed Birk's anger swirling around her, and shot out her hand to keep her childhood Black Knight close to her.

Birk's big, firm hand wrapped around hers and Lacey stopped shivering. A lifted black brow mocked her courage and Lacey braced herself. ''Mother, I got married—''

She held the telephone away from her ear as her mother cursed and yelled. Lacey felt the cold circle her, taking away her breath, then Birk took the telephone, his eyes locked with Lacey's. ''Hello, Jo. Yes, I married Lacey.... Birk Tallchief... Yes, that Birk Tallchief. We've only been married two days.... You, too. Have a nice trip.''

Birk hadn't released Lacey's wrist and when he replaced the telephone to the cradle, he took one look at her and lifted her in his arms.

''I'm a mess,'' she admitted with a sob against his shoulder. ''It's all tangled up.''

He sat, still holding her, and she curled against him. ''You'll be fine, Lacey.''

''I have to do this. To see her again. To make sense of everything. I can do it by myself.''

"Yes, you can," Birk agreed grimly, and gathered her closer. She rested her head on his shoulder as she'd done years before, breathed his soap-and-male scent and leaned back to study him.

One look at the man she'd always known, stilled the restless fear within her. Birk's hand rubbed the back of her head, as he'd done thousands of times before, easing her. "Lacey the lovely," he murmured, a gentle reminder of another time, when they fought dragons together.

Six

"**Y**ou've looked stunned for the entire two weeks you've been married, Lacey. Surely you'd know that once Birk decided you were the one, he'd want to marry you. You married in such a hurry that we wanted to give you a proper bridal shower." Elspeth's sleek black hair gleamed, crossing her Tallchief tartan in a rich braid. A sparkling line of blue beads swayed as she met Alek's kiss. With short curls framing his face and an earring in his ear, Alek also wore the Tallchief tartan. The design mixed Una's Scottish Fearghus plaid with a unique vermillion stripe added by Elspeth's loom.

Elspeth, a professional weaver, had learned from her mother. Una's fiery paisley shawl had brought Elspeth and her husband, Alek Petrovna, together. His sister Talia's marriage to Calum had drawn Alek to Amen Flats.

Amid the tall family of Sioux and Scottish background, Lacey wore the Tallchief colors, a gift to her from Elspeth. She always wore the plaids, had been included in the family, and yet now, she was terrified. While the past clawed at her, the future terrified her.

On a Saturday night, the old Tallchief ranch home, remodeled by Duncan, was filled with townspeople and Tallchiefs. Sybil, Duncan's russet-haired wife, moved gracefully through the seated and standing guests, dressed in an elegantly simple, long black gown. The Tallchief plaid crossed her body, ripening with Duncan's second child. Amid his brothers, Duncan's gaze flicked to his wife, banked desire mixed with love.

Calum lifted his head from the intense discussion when his wife, Talia, passed. Always cool and confident, Calum straightened suddenly and Talia, her long blond hair fanning around her, danced from him. "She's tormenting him," Elspeth murmured with a soft smile. "Since the baby, he's been too careful with her. She just pinched our fair Calum's backside."

Lacey closed her eyes, the old house familiar to her. Matthew and Pauline Tallchiefs' laughter seemed to mix with the steady hum of people talking. She'd almost grown up here, and now everything was different and frightening.

Birk glanced at her, one of those quick, seeking glances, a check mark on her welfare. He'd made it clear that he possessed her—yes, a possession, she mulled. An arm around her shoulder, drawing her near, a kiss and a nuzzle and a lingering caress on her arm. He'd tucked her under his protective and possessive wing, and she didn't like it.

"Elspeth, I don't see why we had to have this shower...when you only got married two weeks ago, and we all were here, just like this, toasting you and Alek after the wedding. There's no reason you should send out invitations and deck out the Tallchief house again. I really don't like celebrations in my—our honor. You even got Fiona to come home in the midst of her battles. It's all so fast," Lacey returned unevenly.

There was Fiona moving through the old friends and never stopping for long. The same age as Lacey and her friend forever, the youngest Tallchief wore her storms and was just as restless as the others. Something nettled Fiona, when the excited homecoming settled, her eyes dark and mulling. It wasn't her current protest, but rather an unrest one woman could recognize in another. She leaped upon her brothers, and the only one without a child locked to him, Birk whirled her around the room. Then he placed his forehead to hers and when they spoke quietly, Fiona quietly laid her head on his shoulder as though she were still a child and at peace for the moment, home with her family.

Only inches shorter than her brothers, Fiona was dressed in the tartan and kilt, her gleaming black hair cut in a sleek practical boy-cut. The family was the same, bound by blood and struggles and by Una's journals. Lacey gripped her cold hands. Another woman should be Birk's wife—opening the gifts and exclaiming to him. *Lacey was a Tallchief, not an outsider, but one of them.*

Lacey ran her shaking hand around her cold face, afraid that she was dreaming. This was the family she'd always wanted, cried to have.

Birk hadn't given her a ring, hadn't wanted the commitment. She hadn't thought about the missing customary ring until now. She hadn't really thought of herself as a wife, bound to Birk, and him to her for anything other than short term. Tonight, they'd opened gifts to share in their new life. Their marriage was only temporary—a dare, a challenge met...and more, he would stand by her as he was expected to do, the Tallchiefs protecting Lacey as they had always done. Lacey shivered, frightened of the leap of her heart just looking at him, his hair gleaming blue-black, his cheekbones jutting beneath the darkly tanned weathered skin, cheeks hollowed and his beautiful, expressive mouth. She'd grown up, used to the smile lurking on Birk Tallchief's lips, and now suddenly, as he turned to her, it seemed so intimate, and just for her.

Lacey rubbed her fingers to her temple, fighting a headache caused by tension and lack of sleep. He'd charmed her like the rest of his harem, and she had to stop looking at him, wanting to touch—

"In comparison to Birk the rogue, dear Alek took his time. And Una's legend of the Marrying Moon came true." Elspeth settled against her new husband, who had led her a merry chase. She looked cool, the familiar Elspeth the elegant, a contrast to Alek's vibrant emotions, his quick laughter.

"I'll leave you two new brides to the discussion of who's the slowest. But there was never a doubt that I'd have you wearing my name, Elspeth-mine." Alek gave his bride a quick, hard kiss and strode off to talk with the three Tall-chief brothers, also dressed in plaids and kilts.

Elspeth's gray eyes traced her tall, broad-shouldered husband, his kilt swaying. "Look at him swagger. I'll have to trim his mountainous pride. He's too cocky by far, still filled with victory after he brought those horses and sheep to Duncan, asking to court me."

Lacey studied the Tallchief males, Calum cradling Kira, his newborn daughter, close, and Duncan with black-haired Megan riding his hip, and Birk— *The maiden who rocks upon the chair and sings a lullaby will claim the man of Fearghus blood who stands closest to her....*

He frightened her. Her need for him, her curiosity about Birk as a lover, frightened her. The past catching up with the future frightened her.

Elspeth took Lacey's hand with her own, just as she'd done thousands of times through the years. "Birk has kept you moving, too busy for us to visit, between working and winterizing your house. You seemed so shocked at the wedding on the mountain and I wanted to wait until you were better adjusted. You've always been special to me, to our family, and it is wonderful that we're all together as a family. I'm pleased that you've married Birk, Lacey. You've always been good for him."

While Elspeth was elegant about her feelings, Duncan and Calum had simply lifted her into their arms and tossed her back and forth, and told her how glad they were that Birk had finally met his match. They'd protected her, the Tallchief brothers, just like they were doing with Emily,

Sybil's daughter, a beautiful flame-haired teenager with boys prowling around her.

Was she Birk's match? Lacey was a miniature when compared to the tall family, whose storms still rode them at times. They strode through life, protecting each other, and carving lives for themselves. When Birk had wanted their sudden marriage ceremony to be up on the mountain, near his parents' resting place, she'd understood. She understood his frustration years ago when the Tallchiefs were trying to hold onto their land, counting the pennies between them for the smallest luxuries. Lacey understood so much about Birk's family, about himself, and yet knew nothing about the man.

He found her with a look that jarred, wary prickles skittering up her spine. She forced herself to calm...was that possible with Birk looking as though he wanted to devour her?

Lacey straightened, her skin prickling, a soft sensuous jolt running deep in her body. Birk had that pointy look that she'd seen his brothers have, when they were hunting their brides. After his track record with tall curvaceous women, she doubted Birk craved her. His current lack-of-female was probably taking its toll.

Lacey traced the brooch securing her tartan, a gift from Alek. With Birk, she was too transparent; she dragged her eyes from his. What would Birk know of her darker side? Of the fear of intimacy and the shame that went with it? She'd held her own, tormenting him—so far.

Gentler storms were stirring in her, unsettling her. He'd kept her busy at home, preparing for the hard winter to come. And after a full workday, she'd come dragging home to him. His light touches, a brush of her hair behind her ear, were familiar, frightening, thrilling.

The elegant old-fashioned tub was always waiting, filled with steam and bubbles for her when she entered the house. Birk was determined that she eat right, and packed her lunches. They would talk quietly as the old house settled down for the night, the wind bringing the fierce winter closer. With her on the couch and Birk lying on the bed, they shared the past, omitting her mother.

"It's all too comfortable, too easy," Lacey muttered as Birk turned to her again in a hard, quick look that sent a jolt to her heart, kicking up the pace. She read the familiar lock of his tall body, the desire heating his eyes and terror spread through her. "What did I do?" she asked herself and found Elspeth's comforting arm around her.

Fanny Butler, almost one hundred years old, and looking for another husband, passed and kissed Lacey's cheek. "Look at you, Lacey. All grown up and married to Birk. I always knew it would happen with you two tormenting each other all these years. Why, I remember when Birk used to ride you around town on his bicycle—you on the back seat, a wee bit of a thing, clinging to that wild adventurous demon. There you'd go, over the hills and taking chances with him that made my heart stop."

Fanny smiled and the beauty of her youth leaped into her face. "I always knew you suited him, because other girls were half afraid of him, the swaggering, arrogant bad boy. You weren't."

Lacey managed a smile. Then Birk found her again and his grim expression made her want to tear into him. The look of him challenged her, made her want to drive him wild, anything but the terror of what she had done by marrying him—possibly ruining his life, definitely changing hers. He'd called her a coward and she'd taken the dare—

Birk eased through the crowd, paused to bend for Fanny's kiss, said something to Fiona, and never looked away from Lacey. She shivered, caught by the heat steaming from her, nerves gearing up. Birk passed Chelsey Lang without a look at her, dressed in a tight black number with a burgeoning, low-cut bodice. Also a friend of Fiona's, Chelsey and half the young women in the room had dated Birk, and yet he kept moving toward Lacey as if nothing could stop him, all broad shoulders, widened by the tartan, his skin dark against the frilled white shirt, and his knees glorious. Lacey swallowed and realized she'd been speaking aloud.

Fiona laughed at Lacey's side. "Most women adore his backside. You're the first to love his knees. They were a mess in high school from football and baseball. He let you play nurse and bandage him and fuss. The rest of us were told to mind our own business. I'm so happy——" Fiona brushed a tear from her cheek. "I've always known this would be, you and him."

"Did you?" Lacey couldn't swallow, her mouth dry, for Birk had not looked aside, on his path to her.

He captured her cold hand and drew it to his lips, smoothing his lips over her knuckles. "Aye," he whispered softly. "You'll do."

The husky timbre of his voice shimmied down her spine, weakened her knees and blurred her eyes.

Fiona and Elspeth grinned. "He's come courting you, Lacey. Watch out," Elspeth, the more experienced of the two sisters advised.

"Are you needing my kiss, Lacey the lovely?" Birk asked huskily, his thumb tracing the dark circles beneath her eyes. He ignored his sisters, and spoke to Lacey as if she were the only woman in the room, in his life. The intimate curl of his deep voice reached inside her, stroking, wooing…while his eyes said he wanted to bed her on the floor. The amused slant of his lips set her off balance. He was the same Birk she'd always known. The one who fitted too perfectly into her life, her home.

He terrified her.

Around the breadth of Birk's shoulders and his tartan, Lacey glanced at the friends and family, their smiles tender and reflecting their own loves. They were a part of her life, and of Birk's. "Don't try to charm me, Birk Tallchief. I'm wise to you," she muttered in a sinking defense. "You're missing your tall, cool ones with curves."

"Aye, you're skimpy, but you'll have to do," he whispered and swooped to lift her in his arms. "To my bride," he announced, standing in the house with the pictures of his family across the mantle, the fire muted in the old rock fireplace. "To my bride," Birk announced again, and took her mouth hungrily as though he couldn't live without her.

He called to something fiery within her, a leaping of her bones to his will, her flesh and skin hungry for him, and Lacey matched his hunger, taking his head in her hands. They broke apart, panting, shaking, heating and wanting more.

"Aye! To Birk's bride!" the other Tallchiefs called with Megan squealing, and Talia—as emotional as her brother, Alek—placed her blond head on Calum's shoulder, nestling to him.

"And now, a few words from my bride. She wants to tell you how lucky she is to have me for a husband...." Holding her high, his hands under her arms, Birk twirled her around once.

She braced her hands on his shoulders, this man who had done her hair when she'd fussed and cried and wanted to hide at home. He'd carried her to his pickup, ignored her pouting and delivered her to the wedding shower held in their honor. She tasted him on her lips, because he'd saved nothing back from the hungry kiss, not sparing her or the crowd. "Let me down, Birk. Or..."

"Or?" he prodded with a grin that stopped her mind from churning.

He looked too confident, as if he'd bested her again, and Lacey ignored caution and consequences, and lowered her lips to his. "If I decided to, I could kiss you mind-less...enough to blow up your skirts—"

He dropped her, and caught her in his arms with the air of old Birk, the show-off, and now he was showing off for her, daring her. Her toes were off the ground by inches, her face on a level with his when he murmured, "You're too late, darling. My skirts are too tight now. I wonder how we'd fit together, you with all that agile softness, quivering to the beat of your heart, and me— Of course, I'm far ahead of you. Let's see how bold you are now after flinging around the house in those catalog scraps, and moaning and panting on the couch.''

The words were for her alone, an intimate testing. It was just a game, a challenge from Birk, waiting for her to throw one back. She was familiar with these rules, comfortable with him. Lacey kissed the intriguing corner of his mouth and whispered, ''Then you'll know that I'm not wearing one of those catalog scraps beneath my blouse.''

Birk's eyes widened. He blinked, and shot a look downward to where her blouse met his shirt. He held her tighter, tried to say something and then with her feet dangling, carried her to the couch and sat.

''You're looking grim, Birk.'' Lacey ran a fingertip around his mouth and let him gather her closer, protecting her. The tension humming in him matched the sudden hardness beneath her hips.

''Sit still,'' he ordered, his eyes flashing at her. He adjusted the tartan to cover her breasts.

''Oh, dear. Have I messed up your pleats?'' she whispered innocently, cuddling closer.

''There's advantages to kilts, darling,'' he returned as the crowd began to murmur again. He stroked the spiraling long curl that had tumbled to her cheek, smoothing it behind the ear he would kiss. ''Shall we step into the closet? Or are you a coward?''

''Necking? With you? You couldn't stand the heat. You'd groan first, Birk Tallchief.''

''We'll see about that. Meet you in the back closet, next to the kitchen, where the winter coats and boots are kept, in ten minutes.'' Birk placed her aside, stretched his arms high over his head and yawned. Ignoring her, he stood and wound around the crowd, accepting congratulations, while she did the same in the other direction.

She found him waiting in the kitchen, his shoulder braced against the closet door, his arms crossed across his chest, and nothing kind in his expression. Kind? She had no intention of being kind to Birk.

''You've been pushing me with those scanty outfits and

moaning from the couch. Let's see just how bold you are now, Mrs. Tallchief. After you, darling,'' Birk murmured, and opened the closet door. A gallant bow taunted her, and lifting her head high, Lacey stepped into the darkness. She could take his dare and up the ante.

"Do you need light—?"

"I know what I'm doing, darling." The amusement in his tone taunted her.

"They'll miss us," she said, unbuttoning her shirt, and tossing away her tartan. No one had ever taunted her like Birk, and the humming within her told her that it was time to strike.

"They expect this of newlyweds, dear heart," Birk returned and as her eyes grew accustomed to the dim light, she saw his face.

The raw hunger should have frightened her—it didn't. It only brought the heat surging out of her, the hunger of her own, need— The button on his shirt popped as he ripped the material aside, flipping their tartans over the rod near his head. "Wouldn't want to damage Elspeth's hard work."

The tiny space pulsed with heat and desire, and Lacey shivered as Birk's finger came strolling down her body, twirling around her breasts. His other hand slid inside the kilt's waistband, to tug her closer. "If we do this right, you'll have to touch me, Lacey."

"Oh, I intend to touch you. When I walk out of here, you'll need a rest before you stagger out, Birk the rogue."

"Threats." Birk nibbled her lips. "We don't have much time before the posse is at the door. Do your damnedest. I'm at your disposal and waiting."

It was no more than play, she thought as her body softened, heated to the slow firm caress of his hands. She trusted him explicitly, trusted him not to hurt her. She shoved away the panic that gripped her when she remembered another dark, small closet— Whatever happened between them, she trusted Birk to stop when she wanted.

The kiss deepened, his hands wandering, caressing, lifting her kilt, smoothing her bottom, and dipping beneath the lace to clasp her close. She pasted herself to him, arched to the height of his hard body, and reveled in the power she felt in his arms.

They were equal now, in the hunger, her hands roaming inside his shirt, threading through the hair on his chest, and catching his head close. She couldn't get close enough, warm enough, in the steam, and lodged firmly against her stomach was a part of him, of Birk the boy she'd known and of Birk the man, who caused her skin to ignite.

His fingers wandered between her thighs, pressing, heating, slid higher and Lacey released the long slow groan she'd been fighting. "Come inside me, Birk," she whispered, humming, throbbing, aching for him.

"It isn't time, but for now this will have to do," he whispered against her hot cheek and bit her jaw lightly. The slight savagery was what she wanted, not the smooth courting he'd used on other women. She dug her fingers into his shoulders and bit his shoulder, muffling the cry of delight as she melted, wilted, laved against him.

Birk shuddered, his hair tangled in her stroking hands. "The sounds you make—"

Lacey's hand moved downward, curious to touch him, to take him in her grasp, this mysterious part of him, that suddenly she knew how to lock within her.

"Don't. Do not touch me," Birk muttered between his teeth, his body shaking as he gripped her wrist.

She held him then, close and safe, and kissed him and eased him gently back from the crest that threatened him. How was it she knew how to touch him, what to say, how to curl against him and lock her arms around him? Yet she knew. She leaned against him and nuzzled his neck, taut with desire, and smoothed his wonderful crisp hair with her fingers.

Outside the closet, Duncan and Calum sprawled at the kitchen table. Calum tossed an olive into the air and caught it in his mouth. "Things are dying down in there. Not so much bumping around and desperate noises."

"He'll have to baby-sit to repay us for standing guard while he necked with Lacey. Every one of the guests must have wanted to come in here for a drink. They would have been shocked if they opened the closet door."

"She needed the distraction. Lacey looked pale and panicked before Birk set after her. Five dollars says she'll be back to normal when they leave the closet, fighting with Birk and lit up like a Christmas tree." Calum flipped another olive high and caught it in his mouth.

"Mmm. Typical overwhelmed bride. It takes us men to settle their nerves," Duncan added sagely, his boot braced upon a chair.

"Ooo. How would we little weak things survive without you big strong men distracting us?" Sybil cooed from the door and batted her lashes. The first guards, Talia and Sybil, stood just outside the kitchen door, and turned to their husbands. Each was holding a big pitcher to refill the drinks, keeping the guests at bay. "Are they—?"

"About finished, dear heart," Duncan murmured, rising to his feet. "Let's clear the place, and send all these orphans home to their own beds."

"Why, Duncan," Sybil purred with a lift of her brow. "Are you wanting me alone?"

Elspeth and Alek entered the kitchen, arms around each other. "So they're in the closet, are they? Who will come out smirking and who will be wearing a black temper?" Elspeth asked. "Will there be any shreds left of Birk the rogue?"

"Maybe they'll both be smirking, Elspeth-mine," Alek purred, defending the honor of his sex, and flipped an olive high.

She caught it, grinned at him, and plopped it in his mouth. "Cocky, aren't you, Petrovna? We'll have to change that."

"Whenever you'd like, heart of my heart."

* * *

Inside the closet, Lacey hurried to button her blouse and smooth her hair. Her hands shook. There was more than sex in the steamy closet, there was intimacy and caring, and the past tangling around her. She shouldn't have cared if Birk ached, after all, that was the wager, who would groan first, and who would make the other pay. She couldn't have acted so hungry with another man—hadn't let one touch her as Birk had. He had her running, and she didn't like it. Birk's hands were far too busy, finding her breasts and lifting them to his lips. She bit off the cry, the beauty of his needs straining against her, and sank her head against the safe harbour of his neck and shoulders. "You'll pay for this, Birk Tallchief. You know very well they are all out there."

"You like to kiss me and you know it. You're not half bad—a little savage when you're aroused." He kissed her nose. "And you were aroused, darling," he pointed out, a score in his favor. "You were ready to lift my kilt—"

"Eat dirt and get serious, Tallchief," Lacey tossed back and pushed away a winter sweater that had fallen to Birk's shoulder. She buttoned his shirt, and adjusted his tartan, smoothing his shoulders and knew that in her heated storm, she'd probably placed marks upon him. She smoothed the peaks in his hair and didn't trust how obedient he was, when she tilted his head for an inspection.

The kilt still protested her smoothing hand, and Birk leaped back, bumping his head against a shelf. While he glared at her, Lacey dusted her hands and stepped out into the brightly lit kitchen to see the Tallchief family gathered around the table, arms around each other, and pleased smiles upon their faces. Lacey stopped abruptly and Birk ran into her backside. She backed against him, digging her back into the security she'd always known. She pushed at her hair, trying to smooth it furiously and knew that her blush told the story. "Say something, Birk."

"That's right, Birk the rogue, tell us why you've corralled Lacey and your button is hanging by a thread." Fiona perched upon the kitchen counter, munching on a buttered slab of Elspeth's freshly baked bread.

Behind Lacey, Birk's hands rode low and possessive on her hips. He peered down over Lacey's shoulder, inspecting her clothing, and carefully adjusted the tartan over her mis-buttoned blouse. "We needed a private discussion," he stated elegantly, as if stepping into closets and sucking each other's lips and throbbing, and melting, occurred every day.

Lacey tried to think—the Tallchief family took in the two of them, and she gripped Birk's wrists. He bent to kiss her hair and nuzzle the tangled wild ringlets.

"He's drunk on love," Duncan stated finally, his arms crossed over his chest.

Love? Lacey whirled to Birk, her heart pounding and the floor caving beneath her feet. She didn't want love of any dimension tangling her life again. "I think this was a mistake," she whispered.

Birk snared an orchid from a design by Alek's father, and artistically arranged it in Lacey's hair. He tucked a delicate bloom over his ear. "There's no mistake, my darling bride. I've got you. You crave me, admit it."

Lacey ignored the laughing family and slowly focused on Birk. Proud of himself, he grinned back at her. He flicked a ringlet beside her hot face and grinned.

There was nothing to do, but to take the pitcher of ice water from Sybil and to pour it down his kilt. Birk stood absolutely still, the water flowing down his kilt to his knees and pooling at his feet. "We should do something about a ring, Lacey. Now that you're committed to making this marriage work," he said sternly, his hands on his hips, while water dripped steadily from the kilt and the orchid gleamed in his hair.

Lacey threw up her hands, issued an "Aargh!" and left the battlefield.

"You're coming along, Birk. I thought she had you with the ice water," Calum said behind Lacey, his tone amused.

"You've always been such a romantic, Birk," Elspeth murmured.

"She looks squashed and hot. You can't pounce on a new bride like that and mess her up at the reception," Fiona called as Lacey marched past her.

"Try candy," Alek offered with a chuckle.

"Thanks, but I'm delectable all by myself," Birk returned, unbothered by his siblings' teasing.

Lacey had enough. She stormed back into the kitchen. Birk looked down at her from his lofty height, his arms crossed over his chest, giving her his best lord-of-the-manor look. She knew in an instant how Tallchief must have looked when Una came back to fight him. Lacey stepped over the water on the floor and punched her finger against his chest. "Don't you dare give me a ring."

"Too late," he returned with a smirk. He took a small box from his pocket, popped it open and flipped a glittering huge diamond in the air. He took Lacey's hand and slid the ring on her finger. "My grandmother LaBelle liked this best, and she should know, since she was the best cat burglar of her time. My grandfather paid for it of course, to save her from jail. He was selfish that way, wanting his wife with him."

There was nothing gentle about Birk's expression, hard determination settling in his jaw, locking it. "It would be hell to dig that out of set concrete. You'll need a plain band. But I'll expect you to wear this when you have our firstborn."

"Firstborn what?" Lacey asked blankly, studying the huge diamond weighting her hand. "This must be—"

"Expensive?" Calum offered.

"I liked the crystals better," she whispered when she could speak and dashed away the tear that came sliding down her cheek.

"I knew she would!" Fiona shouted triumphantly.

"I don't like you at all, Birk Tallchief," Lacey managed, enveloped by her emotions and her uncertainty. For an instant she wished it was true, that Birk would be with her forever and—she let him kiss her, and stood on tiptoe to give it back.

* * *

Holding his gaze, Lacey lifted her chin and flicked open the top button on her frilled shirt, a match to his. The reception was slowing, people leaving, when Birk had carried her outside and plopped her on an unsaddled horse. Duncan had tossed a heavy quilt to Birk and he quickly wrapped it around them both as friends and family sent cheers into the storm brewing on Tallchief Mountain. The newlyweds rode into the night, with the wind dusting light snow against Lacey's face, and Birk's arms warm and strong around her.

Tallchief Lake spread into the night, the storm licking white crests on the water. The pines and firs swayed with the wind that lifted her hair, and cooled her cheeks. On the cusp of November, the wind was biting cold, whipping at her body, and snow clung to her hair—and everything was perfect.

Hand in hand, she moved at Birk's side, making for the clearing along the lake.

The savage night suited him, pleasing her. She'd never felt more alive than when Birk took her prowling in the elements. This was the Birk she knew, the wild, stormy side of him meeting hers, clashing and blending. He dipped under a pine bough, pulling her with him. Suddenly he stopped and tugged her in front of him, wrapping the old quilt around them both.

The wind howled around them, the mountain that reminded Una of Scotland surged up into the night, and with Birk's arms around her, his body warm and strong behind hers, the restlessness settled within Lacey. "This is where you came that night while your parents were new on the mountain, to pledge that you'd find the dowry, and stay together, and lift your thumbs into the night sky—"

Birk took her hand in his and slid it from the quilt. He kissed the scar that had marked her as one of the Tallchiefs, and lifted it into the night with his own. "Aye!" he called into the fierce night, the wind whipping at his hair.

"Aye!" she called, ready to follow him anywhere.

Then Birk whirled her to him, grabbed her flying hair in his fists and took her mouth without a feather of gentleness.

She wanted nothing less than the raw elements within Birk now, and pasted herself to him, giving him more. He drew her so close that nothing could tear her away, anchoring her to him in the wind, and she knew only him, and the savage beating of their hearts. "You'll do," he whispered against her cheek, in a raw deep uneven tone that seemed to come from his very soul.

Seven

Lacey sat on a board, propped between the sawhorses, running her pencil down the checklist in her hand. The project was on schedule; the church board was pleased with MacCandliss Remodeling, which would lead to good referrals and more work. She should have been happy.

Her mind wasn't on work, but on what had happened after the wedding shower. Though LaBelle's ring was safely stored away, Birk had given her a small perfect agate, with a tiny bit of moss trapped inside the delicate pink. A gift from Tallchief to Una, a thin wedding band had been heated, woven to form a tether to the leather thong. Lacey pressed her hand over her chest, finding the stone.

The ceremony on the mountain had been for the Tallchiefs, and the wedding shower for pride and custom. But when Birk had lifted their joined hands to the stormy sky, and called to the wind, "Aye!" he'd given a pledge much deeper. In the savagery of the winter storm circling Tallchief Mountain, her hand locked to his, Lacey had given him much more than she'd intended.

"Aye!" she'd shouted to the wind, blending her promise with his, and she'd given him what he'd wanted. He'd claimed her then, in a kiss lacking patience and skill, but in a raw primitive taking that told her she belonged to him, and maybe she always had.

That was the ceremony, that moment locking them in the cold wind and the warmth rising between them, not the one on the mountain, or anything that had passed before. There was a new look to Birk when he had softened the kiss and looked down at her, the wind whipping at his hair. He had taken her face in his hands and studied her as if he saw straight past her skin, her bones and into her heart. "You're mine now, Lacey the lovely," he'd murmured.

Not to be left behind, she'd pushed her hands through his hair and returned, "And you are mine, Birk the rogue."

But they weren't playing at Black Knights rescuing maidens from dragons, and they weren't children.

Now, in the unfinished church remodeling, Sam Nachman, a subcontractor's electrician, climbed a ladder beside her sawhorses and began connecting wires to a main circuit. Placing her work boots on a wooden spool circled by wiring, Lacey rubbed her glove over her face and jerked off her hard hat. On a Monday morning, pasting a smile on her face while answering congratulations, she could have killed Birk Tallchief. She'd spent Sunday with Fiona and the other Tallchiefs, to heal her raw nerves and tangled emotions. The only thing she could cling to was that she was certain Birk had never unleashed the real storms in him to another woman. She caught that knowledge to her, because she'd always had a piece of Birk that was true, elemental and belonged to no one else. *That moment meant more to him than any of the others—it was Birk's ceremony, out in the wild elements so much a part of his life. Oh, no, he couldn't have chosen a church like Duncan or Calum had, or a ceremony in the middle of Amen Flats like Elspeth had, marrying Alek.* There he'd stood, dressed in the Tallchief plaid, with just the right angle of arrogance to his head, his eyes smoking at her, challenging her. There wasn't an ounce of softness, of romance in him, as he'd tossed his challenge to her.

She'd grabbed him selfishly, for herself, for what she needed, a mate to that same fierce storm within herself. Her high emotions had shocked her then, but not Birk, because he'd laughed, a carefree laugh, tossed to the winds, as if he had what he wanted and it filled him with delight.

She'd returned late, after a Sunday with her new family, revving up her motorcycle, and found Birk working on the old rocker, cherishing it with each stroke of fine steel wool. "Enjoy yourself, darling?" he had asked, the deep tone raising her hackles.

"Immensely. Your family loves me, though I can't say they feel the same about you. Fiona travels light. I took her to the airport on my motorcycle."

Birk had stood, and crossed his arms over his bare chest. He was wearing worn jeans and work socks, and looked as approachable as a grumpy bear just coming out of hibernation. "There are rules to this game, darling, and one of them is that you don't go roaring off on your motorcycle before dawn. There is ice on the roads now, and snow. You'll drive your truck from now on."

As her crew took their morning coffee break, Lacey poured the hot chocolate Birk had prepared into her cup. She brushed back the ringlet that had come loose from her braid. Birk was in a snit and she was feeling—uncertain.

"Can't you keep up?" she'd asked mildly, testing him.

"I had things to do," he'd answered, pushing the rocking chair to her with his foot.

The old chair, brought from Scotland by Una's indentured family, gleamed in rich tones, stripped of the past and rubbed with oil. "It's lovely," she'd whispered, smoothing the old wood that had held Una with her babies upon her lap.

Lacey scowled at the shiny insulation stapled to the church walls and waiting for drywall to cover it. She tapped her boot. Birk wasn't playing by the rules of a temporary situation. After looking so brooding, he'd tipped her face up for a kiss, a light tempting brush of his lips that left her wanting more. "While you girls were giggling and hashing over good times, my brothers and I finished winterizing the house and wrapped the pipes against freezing. The work needed to be done quickly and they needed a place to hide when you girls started crying."

Shifting on her board, Lacey shook her head. Birk had sought the leather thong and followed it to the agate beneath her sweater. Then he'd drawn her slowly to him with the thong. "You're a witch, Lacey Tallchief. And I won't make it easy for you."

Lacey slammed the front door and Birk paused, holding his breath. Then he braced up another board and continued framing in the room. At eleven o'clock in the evening, she'd had time to secure the church remodeling for the night, drop by Maddy's for a beer, and stop at Elspeth's.

He'd known her movements exactly, tracking her through town, because if she hadn't returned soon, he would drag her back and— Elspeth had called Birk later, telling him that he should be nice to Lacey…that Lacey was fighting crying and wouldn't say what bothered her.

Oh, he intended to bother her until she knew just where she should be and who she needed.

Lacey's hard hat hit the floor and her boots sounded against the floor, marching toward him.

She'd hurt him, Birk realized. She'd brutalized his sensitivity as a new groom. He'd planned to keep Lacey for himself, not that he begrudged Fiona's visit, but a telephone call to him, a soft word to tide him over, would have helped.

At his back, Lacey's voice was ominously quiet. "What are you doing?"

"You've remodeled houses, darling. I'm framing in our bedroom."

"No walls, Birk."

He hated the slight tremor of her voice, ached for her,

but continued hammering, framing in the enclosure. "Your mother is coming in two days. I'll need privacy."

And a lock, he thought, remembering Jo's hounding of him and other men. He turned slowly, afraid of what he would see on Lacey's face. Desperation, fear, pain, tore across Lacey's pale face, mirrored in her dark blue eyes, terrifying him. "It won't be so bad, Lacey. It can be removed when she's gone."

Or when I'm removed. The thought ripped through him, freezing him.

"I understand," she whispered too softly. "Yes, privacy. You would need that, a man with two women. I'm used to you, but—"

She said it as though he were an old rug she crossed many times a day. He regretted pushing her farther and put down his hammer. He unzipped her jacket, stripped it from her and knelt to unlace her boots, propping one on his knee. Lacey braced her hand on his shoulder, just as she had when she was years younger. "Correction...*we* need privacy. It's customary for brides and grooms to sleep together."

While Lacey was chewing on that, Birk eased away her jeans and stood to pull her sweater over her head. She understood this part of their relationship worn comfortable by years, yet he wanted more. "If you help, we can add to the outside windows, to make the room seem more open. We'll leave doors off the closet, but a few shelves and a place to hang our clothes wouldn't hurt."

She looked so small and vulnerable, standing there in her thermal underwear. She glanced at the bathtub. "You're right." The words were reluctant, drawn from her as she balanced her fears against practical living.

Birk stroked her cheek, felt the deadly chill move beneath it. "Hey, we're carpenters, aren't we? We can work together, maybe have some of our crews come to help. Walls are nothing but board and plaster that can be removed, Lacey."

"They're damn hard to fight though if you're locked in,"

Lacey murmured unevenly, giving him a small insight into her past.

Her fear of the past echoed on the old walls, cutting into Birk. He wanted to strangle Jo and the man who wasn't Lacey's father. "You don't have to do this, let your mother come here. I could—"

She slashed away his hand. "You're like that, aren't you? Trying to fix my life? Maybe I want to do it myself." She walked to a wall near the bed, picked up a marking chalk and sketched out a line of windows. She sounded the wall, marking the supporting studs and picked up Birk's small power saw, revving it up as she cut a hole in the wall and winter rushed into the old bordello.

"A little unplanned, but serving the purpose." Birk pulled the plug on the power saw she was holding. He slid safety glasses on her head. "Let's do this like the professionals we are, darling."

"Right." Lacey plugged in the power saw, revved it, and began ripping away at the wall as if she could tear it apart with her bare hands.

Birk shook his head and methodically followed her lead, replacing the supports, and framing the window. When a blast of winter wind lifted Lacey's hair, flying around her with sawdust, Birk picked up the telephone and called his foreman. "Buck, I hope you're in a good mood, because I need a home delivery. Get Mel at the lumberyard to open up, will you? We need three windows, big ones—I know it's almost midnight, but we're having a...a family moment."

He sketched out the specifications and studied his wife, a petite woman with a mass of curls flying in the wind. Dressed in her thermal underwear, and wielding a small power saw, Lacey was fighting her demons.

At one o'clock in the morning, Lacey had stopped only for the mug of soup Birk had pressed into her hands. The windows were in place, keeping the wind outside, and a blanket had been hung over them for privacy. "There," Lacey said, dusting her hands. "That's all there is to that."

"Not quite. Come here and kiss me to celebrate," Birk said, placing aside the broom he'd been using to sweep up the sawdust. She looked as if she'd collapse at any minute, sawdust caught in her hair and thermal underwear.

"You're feeling broody, aren't you? Because I stole your macho spotlight, the big moment when you sweep in and save little helpless me. You're far too arrogant, Tallchief. It's my house, and I wanted to—"

"I know…do it by yourself." Birk stripped off his T-shirt and socks, tossing them into a corner. Someday, Lacey might let him into her locked corners. "I deserve a medal," he muttered, tearing off the plastic sheet that had been protecting the bed.

"That's not my bed," Lacey stated, blinking at the big old-fashioned four-poster that Birk had widened and lengthened to suit him.

"Your bed is upstairs for your mother. By the way, she'll need a bathroom too—for privacy." And because he didn't want Jo walking in on him, or sharing Lacey's soap. He wrapped his hand around her neck, smoothing the delicate line. "You're tired, dear heart. You've got shadows under your eyes. You'll probably be so tired tomorrow that you won't have the energy to invest in those sexy telephone calls to me, will you?"

She grinned up at him, too tired to notice that he'd been unbuttoning her thermal wear. "That was a stroke of genius and payback for how you treated me at the shower. I was improvising. I did much better on the second one, don't you think? How did you like the rhythmic panting, slower, then picking up, just a bit louder at the end and then…that final sound was a masterpiece, don't you think? Like the cherry on top of a sundae?"

After the first call, he couldn't walk, his body hard and aching for her. After the second, he knew how really tempting Lacey could be when she wanted to charm a man. He didn't want her tempting any other man. He had snapped at his men, told the board chairman of the school to mind his own business, and had almost gone to claim his wife.

"The part where you groaned rhythmically, getting louder as you panted must have been difficult to manage with all the workmen around. The background sound of power saws and men yelling was a distraction."

"You sound miffed, Tallchief."

"I understand two of your men went home for emergencies and came back smiling." He tugged off her socks, her thermal underwear, and ran his fingers around the elastic and lace she wore around her hips. The triangular lace covering each breast was smooth beneath his fingertips. "Afraid?"

Before Lacey could move, Birk picked her up and carried her to the tub, foaming with bubbles. With Lacey pounding nails as though she were killing the past, he'd had time to run water into the tub. He gently lowered and dropped her into the water and while she struggled and flopped and prepared to yell, he stripped away his jeans and shorts and eased into the tub behind her. When she began to curse, Birk calmly stripped the lace from her. "Lean back, Lacey and relax."

"I'll kill you," she purred with a luxurious sigh.

"Mmm. Keep squirming like that, and I'll let you."

Lacey held very still as Birk soaped her back and her arms. The tension changed to sighs and she eased back against him, right where he wanted her, safe and with him. "Sleepy?"

"You're very good, Tallchief. You've probably done this a million times before, but tonight I just don't care. You'll smell like flowers tomorrow and your men will call you Lavender and Musk."

"If they do, I'll give them a kiss."

She giggled at that and nestled her back against his chest, settling into him. Birk inhaled sharply as she turned to him, placing her arms around his neck and snuggling down upon him. "You're not so bad," she whispered drowsily. "Same old, same old Birk."

"I've changed a bit," he murmured against her lips and ignored Gizmo's low growl.

When she was thoroughly limp and drowsy, Birk
propped up Lacey to her feet and stepped from the tub to
dry her. He slid his T-shirt over her head and carried her
to the bed. Dennis and the rest of the cats were waiting on
the bed, mildly protesting as Birk eased Lacey into it.
"Sleep by me, Birk," she murmured, already drifting off
and curled to her side.

He inhaled, skimmed the curves beneath the blankets,
and shook his head. Then, because he had no choice, he
eased into the bed and curled around Lacey, drawing her
back to him. Her bottom nestled into his lap and Birk shook
his head grimly, forcing himself to drift into sleep.

Lacey washed her hands over her face, gripped her mother's heavy suitcase and lifted it from the back of her pickup.
Through the window, Birk noted that Jo MacCandliss
hadn't changed, a petite woman with eyes like Lacey's, and
there the resemblance stopped. Years had hardened Jo,
though she dressed youthfully and chose her cosmetics
carefully. She studied the old bordello, noting the improve-
ments Lacey had made. Dollar signs ran through her hard
blue eyes.

Home for lunch, and worried about Lacey, Birk jammed
dirty clothes into the washer, threw in soap and softener,
and hurried out the door. He passed Jo as she held out her
traveling makeup case to him, and reached to take the
heavy bag from Lacey. He wrapped his arm around her,
glad that hers encircled him. Her body hummed with tension.

Whatever had been said, in the short distance from the
bus stop, it had drained Lacey. "I should have sent more
money. The bus trip was too hard on her."

"Hello, Jo," Birk managed, not bothering to wrap his
greeting in warmth. Lacey had that guilty, haunted look he
remembered and hated.

"So you married Lacey, did you?" Jo wandered around
the airy space, picking at the Tallchiefs' wooden baby
spoons, and grimacing at the clutter of boards and sawdust

against the new walls. "You have a construction crew, and Lacey has a few men working for her. I would have thought that you could afford a real house."

Birk wanted to tell Jo that she could keep her thoughts to herself, but instead he said, "This is Lacey's home."

"She always was stubborn, and making things hard.... The animals will have to go," Jo noted, pulling aside her expensive winter coat as the herd approached her. Gizmo showed his teeth, and plopped himself in front of Lacey.

The dog showed promise, Birk decided, because Lacey had just shuddered. "They never go upstairs, and that's where you're staying. I'll take your bags up now."

With the ease of a selfish person fending for her needs, Jo opened the refrigerator and prowled through it, taking a can of beer and slapping a sandwich together. She pivoted to Lacey. "You could get a nice dollar out of this place and get something cozier."

She sidestepped Gizmo, the cats, and sat on the arm of the couch, studying Lacey as she ate, "I said, you could get a nice price from this. You remember that my owner-ship in the old place got you started, don't you? Part of MacCandliss Remodeling rightfully belongs to me. And this house, of course."

Birk remembered how, without Lacey knowing it, the Tallchiefs had spent hours to find a loophole in the deed, maneuvering the title into Lacey's name.

There was pride in Lacey now, as she braced her body, digging in against her mother and said, "You'll get your money back. I like this. This is my home. I rebuilt it my-self."

"It's been something like eleven years since I saw you, and you are just as stubborn. You'll change your mind. I'm going upstairs to nap now. I hope I have a bed. I'd think you'd want something better for my daughter, Birk." Jo's heavily mascaraed eyes drifted lazily over Birk, dressed in his work clothes and boots. "You still have that raw, prim-itive look that appeals to women. No wonder I was attracted to you."

Lacey stood very straight, her body locked, her fists tight, as her mother ascended the stairs. Then she turned to Birk, her lips tight. "Do I remind you of her, is that it? Am I her replacement?"

He wanted to show her that he loved her, and it had nothing to do with Jo MacCandliss. "I think that you have had a long day already, and it's only noon."

Tears gleamed on Lacey's lashes, her mouth trembling. "You should know. You had me flattened to the bed this morning, and not a stitch between us. 'Wake up, Lacey, and play,' you said, kissing me before I was awake. I wouldn't have kissed you, given an even start. I wouldn't have let you—" She blushed and Birk knew that for the moment, Lacey wasn't unnerved by her mother. "Don't ever suck my toes again, Birk Tallchief."

"I wanted you frothing, thinking about me all day, a payback for the steamy telephone calls." Her focus was exactly where he wanted it, on what was happening between them. He touched the tip of her breast and it hardened as Lacey gasped.

"I intend many, many more. Much worse. You'll be drooling and mindless when I finish with you," she threatened.

"Then you'll have to take the consequences, won't you?" Birk asked, and wrapped his arm around her. He smiled grimly to himself, when Lacey patted his bottom and ran out to her pickup, soaring off to work. She'd hammer and yell at her men, and work into the night, and at least he knew she'd be safe.

Birk had intended to wait for his talk with Jo, but now, after seeing Lacey, white and shaking, fighting desperately for her future, he saw no reason to spare her mother.

"Let's get the rules straight, Jo," he said a few minutes later, his shoulder braced against an upstairs beam.

He lifted her clothes strewn across the rocker, and watched her sprawl upon the bed, smoking and careless of the wrapper around her. He tossed her clothes to the bed and she kicked them to the floor.

"Is this the part where the territorial Tallchief makes his stand, against little old me? Lacey is tough, Birk. I taught Lacey everything and she owes me."

Birk noted that Jo did not call Lacey her daughter this time. "That's not the way I see it."

"She doesn't know anything about being a woman. Look at her. She's little more than the tomboy she's always been. You married her to get her remodeling business and this place. People love restored historical buildings, and you know it. They look at old buildings and see bed and breakfasts, big families and whatever. I see work."

"Exactly why did you come back, Jo?"

She blew smoke into the air. "By law, Lacey is my daughter. I almost died giving birth to her. I'm down on my luck and she owes me."

"Uh-huh. You tried to get rid of her too late in your pregnancy."

"How this town does talk. But then you Tallchiefs always had everything sewed up, people taking your sides. No wonder I kept the one kid and farmed out the rest with that mother of yours—"

Birk gripped the back of the old rocker. "'One kid'? You had more?"

She slashed her hand, dismissing other children. "They were accidents, before I got smart—" She stopped when Birk shoved away from the beam. "I'm back and Lacey wants me here," she said in a too sweet tone.

Farmed out the rest. Birk decided not to push Jo, just yet, but to put Calum on the trail of Lacey's potential other brothers or sisters. Lacey would want to know. "Then we'll have to get along, for Lacey's sake, won't we?" Birk asked, taking the cigarette from her mouth and dropping it into the opened can of beer. "Lacey doesn't like smoking in her house. I'm going back to work."

He picked up the chair and carried it downstairs to the bedroom he shared with his wife. He wished protecting Lacey was as easy.

* * *

Two days of her mother caused Lacey's stomach to knot. She studied the plans for the church's built-in bookshelves, checking the framing measurements, and consulted the cabinetmaker. She wondered if her headache would last forever, and wondered how she would pay for her mother's charge accounts in Amen Flats. She wondered how she would make the payroll and dismissed the call from the real estate agent who had heard she'd be selling her home.

She plopped onto the floor, put her head on her knees and wished she hadn't awakened to a terrified cry—and found it was her own. Lacey rubbed her temples. Her mother was definitely interested in Birk, and Lacey knew that he was putting on an act for her mother, playing the new and well-satisfied husband. Yet something ran between Birk and her mother, and Lacey couldn't bear to think that she was her mother's replacement.

Lacey washed her hands over her face and shook her head, the sound of the hammers and saws beating against her. Her mother had been wary, circling her, and finally asked if Birk had told her anything…"Anything about other kids?"

Lacey retraced the old arguments and realized with the horror of an adult, that the possibility was there for other children.

A boot nudged her bottom, and in the next minute, Birk had lifted her in his arms, carrying her out to the scaffolding. "Are we going somewhere?" Lacey asked, and realized how much she'd missed him since breakfast.

"Afraid?" The slant of his head, the dark look in his eyes challenged her. "It's lunchtime. We're going to the drive-in for hamburgers. You can sit close to me. Maybe on my lap. I'll let you feed me, and you can tell me how you're feeling. You can tell me what kind of roses we should plant in Lil's old garden."

"It's a lovely old garden. We'll have to build a trellis." Lacey placed her hand on Birk's cheek. He was good for her, making her feel alive, and somehow very new.

Birk stopped, still carrying her. Something shifted inside

her then, softened, and she lifted her lips to brush his. "What was that for?" he asked unevenly.

"You're not getting much out of this, Birk. All those needs, unmet and aching? The revved-up harem waiting for your return?"

"I have what I want." He slid her into the pickup and started the motor. He shot her a look that challenged and teased. "Come sit by me, Lacey the lovely. You're too far away."

"Birk—" She gave way to her needs and threw her arms around his neck.

His mouth fused with hers, just like she wanted, offering her heat and comfort and challenge.

Lacey awoke after midnight, a terrified cry locked in her throat. There were walls all around her, the moonlight sliding through the windows without drapes. Upstairs, her mother's radio was playing, as it had been when she was a child. She pushed off the blankets, remembering the confinement, and Birk's arm settled around her. He gathered her closer to him. There was no mistaking his arousal brushing her thigh, or the drowsy purr as he whispered, "You're here with me, Lacey. Una's rocking chair is in the corner and the cats and Gizmo are sleeping in the basket on the floor. The door is unlocked and you can walk out at any time."

She listened to the quick beat of her heart, the fear racing through her. "I've got to settle this," she whispered, shaking as he brought her hand to his mouth.

"You will. You've done all the right things so far. You've tried to communicate. You've tried to understand. You'll make the right decisions." Birk spoke with a confidence that she did not have, as if he knew that she would sort out the past, settle it. He drew her over him and grinned, shifting the mood. "I always thought wives wore sexy little numbers to stir up interest, not thermal underwear with socks."

"I believe you are stirred," Lacey reminded him, the

terror shredding and easing away. She had Birk pinned beneath her and his slow, wicked grin sent her a challenge she could not refuse. "I think I could tame you, just like Una tamed Tallchief, if I wanted. Not that I want to, but if I wanted to put you in your place."

He toyed with her hair. "I'd stop the sexy phone calls, if I were you."

"Can't take it?"

"Mmm." Birk shifted her upon him and settled his hands on her backside, caressing her hips as the bed creaked pleasantly beneath him. "Trapped in a bordello beneath my wife. Now what would I be thinking about? This?"

Birk rolled over, taking her beneath him. "This is the order of things, Lacey Tallchief. Males dominate submissive females." His hand skimmed down her curves, lingered on her thigh, caressing the softness. "You don't qualify for a Black Knight."

"Submit, Birk the rogue, or I'll play dirty," she tossed back in the familiar game. She kissed him with what she'd learned from him, the slow sensuous kiss, a nibble on his lower lip, a bite on his chin and a flick of her tongue against his ear. When he was simmering nicely, she sat up, turned on a lamp, and picked up a sexual manual. While Birk lay next to her all rumpled and heated and her nerves quivered with his hot look, Lacey practiced the sounds of an aroused woman about to climax. Then she snapped the book shut, turned off the light and flopped back on her pillow. She grinned at his scowl. "Steaming yet, darling?"

"It's definitely warmer in here."

Eight

"Mother, your call said you had an emergency?" Lacey's cool tone set the hair on the back of Birk's neck rising.

He eased Jo's arms from around his neck, forcing her wrists down. Over Jo's head, Lacey's expression was grim, taking in Jo's loose robe and Birk's rumpled hair. He knew exactly how the scenario looked, how Jo had intended it to look, just four days into her visit. "Lacey, this isn't—"

"She knows what it is, Birk," Jo cooed, stroking his chest and sending him a sultry look beneath her mascaraed lashes.

Birk leaned back against the kitchen counter, where Jo had pinned him before Lacey opened the door. He braced his hands on the counter, and in his frustration wanted to tear it apart. He studied Lacey. Would she believe him? "Your mother called me and said she was hurt."

Jo smirked. "And you were only too ready to begin our affair again."

Lacey's cool gaze slid to him and back to her mother, who allowed the silky robe to open, revealing the slope of one breast and her thighs. "I'd just come out of the tub and here he was—ready. You really should keep him satisfied, Lacey."

Jo's eyes slashed to Lacey, her voice cutting like a knife. "We were involved years ago. He wanted me and now, I realize he still does. The Tallchiefs always were uppity, but I knew when he wanted me. We had an affair—he's a lusty one, despite how he acts with you, and now—" Jo shrugged, eyeing Birk. "I suppose he wants to start again. It was me he wanted all along. Anyone can see you don't know enough to keep him satisfied."

Birk sucked in air, his chest hurting from lack of it. He'd been very careful with Lacey, especially around her mother. Would Lacey believe him?

Lacey flicked him a glance, the lift of her chin told him she'd already judged the play and found him guilty. Birk sucked in another breath and crossed his arms over his chest. He focused on his boots, braced against the fist that had just slammed into his gut and knew that nothing could hurt him more than the lack of Lacey's trust. Jo had set the stage beautifully and he looked guilty as hell. Lacey had seen enough of her mother's liaisons…a man had his pride. He'd move out, let her chew on the facts, and—a knife slashed across his chest, his fingers digging painfully into his arms. *Oh, Lacey, baby. I'm sorry for this, but a part of me understands.*

"Mother, I've tried to make peace with you. You've been here three days and you want me to sell my home. I won't. But I will check on your claim to my property. I will pay off the accounts you've charged in my name, because the people of Amen Flats are my friends and I won't have you damaging the Tallchief name or pride. They'd pay for your charges, but you are my problem and not theirs. I'll give you enough for bus fare and a week's rent wherever you decide to land. You should be able to get a job by then."

Or another man, Birk added, the vise around his chest easing. Hope trickled down on him like glistening April raindrops, because Lacey had chosen to believe him. The slash to her tone, the fierce pride in her expression took his heart soaring. Oh, she was a part of him and he of her, like thunder and storms, and quiet nights and moon drops. He allowed himself to go slightly woozy, releasing the fear.

There she stood, his wife, his Lacey the lovely. Overmatching the woman she'd battled in her dreams, digging in her heels, and grasping the future with her two fists. He'd cherish this sight for all his lifetime, the high temper of his wife.

"You owe me!" Jo screamed when her lips stopped opening and closing.

"No, I don't." Lacey spoke too quietly, prowling through the square of daylight crossing into her home. The same petite build as her mother, Lacey faced Jo. Her eyes, as blue as her mother's, but now a darker, more dangerous shade, narrowed. "Not at this stage of the game. I thought I did. I saw you as someone who grew up without the support that the Tallchiefs gave me. I hoped to make a difference, make it up to you. I've made a life for myself, built it from nothing, except the lie that you were dead. I've tried to help you and it isn't working. You'll have to decide to do it yourself—"

"Those interfering Tallchiefs! I—" Jo lifted her nails to slash and Birk shoved away from the counter, ready to defend Lacey.

Fast with her hands, Lacey stuck one firm finger to his chest, detaining him; her other hand grabbed her mother's wrist. Muscles gained by lifting and straining and hard work, detained the older woman. "I love the entire Tallchief family. I made mistakes and they were always there."

Lacey lifted her chin, and braced her feet, exactly as she did when she wasn't budging. Birk reveled in the fierce price, that as a woman, she could hold her own. Lacey turned to him, dismissing her mother's furious expression and curses as she rubbed her freed wrist. No longer wounded from the past, Lacey had determined to close it. "That's right, Birk. I tried to help her because I thought—

never mind. You are going back to work now and letting me handle the rest of this. It won't do for both of us to be behind at work. We'll talk tonight.''

Birk glanced at Jo who was flexing her nails as if she'd launch herself at Lacey. He ached for what Lacey must have seen as a child— "I think I'll stay."

Lacey pivoted to him, her body taut, and eyes flashing. She'd pulled herself up to every inch of her five-foot-three-inch height and seemed taller. "I can manage, thank you," she murmured. "Don't you have something to do?"

News in Amen Flats traveled fast and said that Lacey had packed her mother on the next bus.

She'd be packing him next, Birk brooded, and threw himself into framing the new room in Lacey's house. Dressed only in loose undershorts, Birk almost chewed the nails he'd been holding in his mouth as he hammered. She hadn't come home from work yet, and the clock was approaching eleven. She'd called Calum, asking him to define her mother's interest and make arrangements for any due payment. Birk had made calls, finding that she had visited the lumberyard and the drugstore. She hadn't cared enough to call and tell him where she was, or when she would return, and he had crossed from dented pride into a fine steaming temper. "I'll hunt her down and make her listen...and then she can throw me out."

Gizmo made a good listener, tilting his head as Birk muttered and hammered and brooded. When Lacey had ordered him back to work, his instincts had told him to stay. It had cost him a measure of pride to nod and walk out the door.

That door slammed open and Lacey waltzed in, tossing her hard hat onto a chair. She crouched, gathering her herd to her. Birk placed aside his hammer and jerked off his leather gloves, his hands trembling as he removed the nails from his mouth. She looked too tired and drawn, her cheeks reddened from the whipping wind. She should have eaten hours ago and he should have stayed— "Working over-time?" *Or staying away from me?*

She walked past him, carrying her backpack, on her way to the bathroom. "I had to take time off, in the middle of the day. Lumber didn't come in, the linoleum had a flaw in it—we'll have to reorder—and the paneling didn't match. Other than that, everything is just peachy and on schedule. The congregation will be able to hold Christmas services, minus a few window dressings, in their own church. I'm taking a bath."

Just like that. Lacey had dismissed him, like so much dirty laundry. Birk inhaled, ready to defend himself and then decided that he'd wait until she'd calmed down—the hell he would. Birk jerked open the door to the bathroom and found Lacey already in the steaming shower, washing her hair.

"Don't you know that there is a thing called 'private space'? Get out," she ordered, too coolly, and setting him off.

Birk opened the shower door and scowled at his petite wife, who shoved wet hair from her face and glared back. "Good. I was hoping you'd make this difficult. I'm used to difficult from you, anything else would—"

"Remember whose shower you're in, bub," Lacey snapped.

So much for quiet, meaningful discussions, and resolving the past together. He lifted her from the shower and ran a towel over her, wrapped up her hair and stuffed her arms into an old flannel robe she wore in the mornings. More than once, he'd caught it close and smelled the scent right out of it, waiting for her, and the thought left him no pride. "'Private space.' If you're going to order me out of your life, you can damn well face me to do it. So you can do everything by yourself, can you?" he asked grimly, rubbing the towel over her head, despite her protests.

He flung it away and brushed the length of curls, with her braced between his legs and squirming as she had as a child. A tangle must have hurt because she eyed him as though she wanted to peel his skin away, in strips. She was angry, was she? So was he, furious with himself for wanting more than she could give. Desperate for one tiny dram of female wiles that told him she cared. "Hold still."

"I can do everything…anything. All by myself. You forgot something." There wasn't an ounce of give in Lacey. She reached past him for a bottle, squirted a liquid in her hand and quickly rubbed it in her hair, whipping the brush through her hair as she glared at him.

He caught the old robe's lapels and drew her to him. "I want to know what happened."

"How like you to prowl through my life, digging at it, tracking me. Everyone thinks Duncan and Calum are thorough, but they don't hold a match to you. And you're not that easygoing. You're prickly and sensitive one minute and teasing the next," Lacey stated haughtily and tore away from him. She grabbed the backpack, and ran into the bedroom.

He didn't want another night of Jo between them. Birk pushed open the door, with Lacey braced against it. A rug caught on her heel and sent her sprawling on the bed. He gripped the door, because he wouldn't slam it. He wouldn't—Birk slammed the door. "I did not have an affair with your mother."

There, he'd said what had been broiling his brain and causing his hands to shake, that and the fear that Lacey would never talk to him again. "We can still be friends."

He caught the long line of her legs, and the shimmering curves of her breasts as she scampered to her feet and tossed away the possibility. He wanted more. Only pride kept him from admitting that he wanted to drag her close and fill his senses with her.

Lacey hugged the robe close to her. "I'm not telling you the details, Birk. My mother and I sorted things out. I'm expecting to hear from her once in a while. But I know now that I could never be like her. Because I'm changing my life and that's it. She has to make her own decision to change. And I am finding my brother and sister, the ones she gave away before me.''

''It's true, then—''

''I will take care of it, but now you are on the discussion menu.'' Lacey glared at him, the towel turbanned around her head and wet tendrils coiling down her cheek. ''Friends won't do, between us, Birk. Because I have plans to seduce you, Birk Tallchief. My mother won't be here to protect you. Now get out of here and let me do my business.''

She jabbed her finger in his chest and Birk, winded, backstepped out of the room. She believed him. He had a reputation with women, her mother had set up the scene, and…Lacey believed him. While he reeled with that, Lacey slammed the door in his face. He plopped down on the nearest chair and stared at the door. ''Do you believe me?'' he called, still stunned.

She answered him impatiently, ''Do you need it in writing? Would I be going to all this trouble, if I didn't?''

Birk sat up, suddenly not tired, or frustrated or winded. He cycled through what Lacey had said to him. ''Did you say 'seduce me'? As in, have me?''

Behind the door, Lacey muttered to herself. ''I'd say we're past schedule and if there is anything I hate, it's being off schedule. I learned a long time ago that schedules make things work. Now I'm tired, I'm emotional, and it's been a long, long day. I'd like to cover all my bases in one day and get everything out of the way. Seducing you is the last thing on my list. I've already made out the payroll.''

Birk grinned. He'd planned a seduction, planned to woo Lacey into a permanent arrangement, after her mother was gone. But Lacey, true to form, had leaped on ahead of him. Birk thought of a proper honeymoon, and a long very warm winter. ''Typical. What's the time frame? And do you expect overtime?''

Lacey swung open the door, dressed in a tiny black peignoir with scraps beneath it. The lamp behind her showed every curve. Her work boots, unlaced and dotted with cement, added an uncommon effect, more erotic than slippers.

She took a deep breath that lifted the tiny black bra and walked toward him slowly, all long legs and curves and scents that— Birk lurched to his feet, no small task when lust had just speared him in the gut.

She may have sounded businesslike and determined a heartbeat ago, but now she faltered and Birk's heart began to spin. "You're going to make me come all the way, aren't you?" she asked when he didn't move.

"All the way," he repeated, his throat drying at the sight of her. "Is this more modeling? More teasing?" If it was, he'd turn into stone.

She ran her finger down his bare chest. "I'm trying to tempt you. And don't look so confused. I'm certain you've got enough experience to do the job."

Birk shuddered, and wondered if he'd had any experience. Lacey's impending seduction of him left him feeling about to be plucked. "I don't suppose you're going to make this easy."

Lacey wrapped her arms around him. "I never intended to make anything easy for you, Birk, and I'm not feeling sweet. You've never failed me, when I needed you."

He traced the fine line of her eyebrows and down her nose and across her lips. "So you just swagger in here late at night and let me know that it's seduction time, is that right?"

"I had to shop. You can't believe the amount of time it takes. Getting the druggist to open and shopping for lotions and oils and powders, and perfume sampling isn't easy when you're still smelling glue from flooring." Lacey settled against him. "I think old Art really enjoyed helping me choose."

"He would. He probably won't sleep all night." Birk struggled valiantly to set the rules, and then slid his hands beneath Lacey's bottom, caressed the softness, and gently lifted her higher. When Lacey stepped into his life, rules didn't apply.

She wrapped her arms and legs around him. "When I was little, you used to carry me like this."

Birk glanced down at her breasts nuzzling against his chest, and wondered how he could walk; his body was one long, hard ache. "Times have changed."

"I still feel safe. Like I have my own Black Knight of the Tallchiefs and nothing will go wrong, wherever he takes me." Birk groaned when Lacey nuzzled the spot behind his ear and whispered, "I think there is something you should know—only because you're so sensitive and you'd be angry later, if I didn't tell you. But you've got to promise not to be shocked, and if you laugh at me, I'll kill you."

Birk gathered her closer. She was so incredibly Lacey, all warm and soft and fragile and sweet. Her legs tightened around him, and Birk added desirable and mysterious to the list. "I won't laugh."

She toyed with his hair, and inspected his ear, then slanted him a wary look. "Well, there's this little matter of my being a virgin— See? I knew you'd be shocked. When you're really shocked, you stop everything and dig in, like you have to get your bearings before you can move. You just stopped walking, and I knew what you thought of me. I tried to get rid of it, but somehow no one seemed to...appeal. It's an intimate thing, you know. I let those men brag, because it suited me. I was pretty close once or twice, but you or your brothers turned up and dragged them off me. I really didn't like your lectures, if that's what you call yelling, or your interference. I liked being Racey Lacey for a time."

Somehow he wasn't shocked. He'd expected anything, but he decided to have a chat to clear the air with the men who had boasted about his wife. Not a brawl, as he would have liked to, but more of an understanding.

Birk reeled in the knowledge that Lacey desired him, wanted him. While desire slammed at his body, a gentler emotion curled around his heart. "You can tell me to stop and I will."

"Aye, I know and you'll probably yell at me again. That's what you do, yell at me." Her look flirted, challenged and tempted. "That is why you're perfect seduction material. I understand your moods. You're experienced, and I can trust you.''

''That's a neat checklist.'' Still reeling with her latest news, Birk's knees weakened when she sent him a look that invited and heated.

He began walking slowly to the bed, while Lacey's intuitive little tongue toyed with his ear. She nibbled on his lobe and whispered, ''You're shaking. I'll bet I've scared you. Any time you want to stop, just let me know. And you can yell, if you want.''

''You're shaking,'' Birk whispered against Lacey's naked breast.

Lacey released the bedpost she'd been holding, and forced her teeth from her bottom lip. She let out a long, devastating sigh. ''How long does this part go on?'' she asked, desperate for Birk to become a part of her body. She tried to sound matter-of-fact and offhand...no small thing when her body had flowed through his hands, when she'd bitten his shoulder to stop from crying out at the pleasure swirling around her. Would she ever forget his scent, the dark, stormy, hungry sweep of his eyes down the body he had just bared? Her valiant ''I'm ready now,'' came out husky, uneven and seductive. ''Surely you've had enough playing. Go on to the next part.''

If he didn't stop...didn't proceed...she'd burst, flying apart.

''Not near enough playing. This isn't an engine we're putting back together, or a room we're building. The play is by intuition. But I'd say we're getting there.'' Birk's smile moved along her belly, coursed up to the taut, aching tip of her breast and he nipped her. He eased over her, and settled lightly upon her, forearms braced along her head, his fingers toying with her hair.

He was too pleased, the lazy curve of his mouth destroying her. Lacey fought panting, fought screaming, and glared up at him. She was losing control, because the panting continued on, in spite of her determination. She kicked away

the sheet that had come between his legs and hers. She
wanted nothing to interfere with her taking of Birk Tallchief. "You're taking your own sweet time."

"I can't allow myself to be plucked like a juicy apple,
can I? You wouldn't appreciate me, if I did." Birk's teeth
slid along her jaw and down her throat. The bed creaked
as he shifted, sliding his hands down her body, stroking her
thighs. But there was nothing lazy in his demand, a fierce
taut proud demand, that let her know he couldn't be had
easily. "Say you want me, Lacey. Say it."

Easy? Birk had never been easy, despite his teasing and
seductive kisses. The challenge was always there, begging
her to leap at him, to prove that she could hold her own.
Now, he dared hold himself from her, and he was the prize,
his will matched against hers. Her pride slipped a notch
and in another moment she'd be begging. She tried to
stiffen her thighs, to stop them from quivering. Cradling
Birk's hard body, they quivered on to each stroke of his
hands, despite her will. "You're determined to take your
time about this, aren't you? I never should have told you
that you would be the first. Of course, I want you. Maybe
I always have."

She loved his roguish grin, the delight in his eyes. "I
knew it. Because I'm delectable and charming." His hands
slid under her body, lifting her gently, a contrast to the
demanding pressure of his mouth, the rhythmic thrust of
his tongue. "Open for me, Lacey."

She dug her fingers into his back, anchoring him to her,
luxuriating in the flex of muscle and the smooth skin covering it. He wasn't leaving her, not until she had her fill of
him. And now, she wondered if ever she would. "I'm going
to burst and you're playing games. Yes...yes, damn you, I
want you."

"Mmm. That sounds good. So sweet. You're learning."
Birk eased slowly down on her and Lacey braced her hands
on his chest.

"Tell me if you want to stop," he murmured, shaking

against her and taking her one step further to where she wanted to go.

Stop? Could spit put out a forest fire? *Stop?* Maybe another time, when she wasn't dying for him. She could depend on him. Birk Tallchief was who she had waited for, who she wanted to enter her body. She had chosen him long ago. "Come here," she whispered to his lips, delighting in the heavy pressure of his body upon hers, in the beat of their hearts racing together.

She hadn't expected the shattering pain, crying out with it, pushing away from him.

"Lacey...." Birk's tone was raw with frustration, and caring for her. His tall body shook violently within the clasp of hers and he held still, wiping a tear away from her cheek. "I'm sorry. I didn't know. God, you're shaking."

"Give me a minute. I'll get back with you." Lacey closed her eyes and found the pain easing.

He looked so pained, so terrified, and shocked and dazed that Lacey had to kiss him, a battery of small kisses along his lips and over his cheeks, and in her heart, she knew she would have to woo him back to her, to where they would go. Schedules, she thought, depending on them, and the one she had in mind for Birk tonight. She lifted her hips to his, taking him fully, stretching, aching, needing, heating.

Birk shivered, his features gaunt, his hands trembling as they touched her softness, tracing her shoulders, her arms, her hands. They were hard, firm hands, lined with calluses and the past. The rest of him was new, invading her body, filling her. "You're so small. I should have—" The raw whisper had been torn from him, his body shaking, his features sharpened.

She leaned into his hands, his fingers rubbing her head. "I could lie with you forever like this," she whispered, her hands smoothing the muscled power of his hips, flowing over the magnificent creature who was more in her power, than she was in his. Or was it an even match? She preferred to think that given time, she could catch up with him. She angled her head to look past his shoulder, down the hard, smooth angles of his long body.

His smile curved along her throat. "You know you want to look. Go ahead."

Of course she did, she wanted to see how he fitted to her, how could his larger body fit hers so completely. She lifted, curious now, and Birk groaned as her hips rose in the movement. "When you were twelve and I was six, I watched you skinny-dip in the lake. Even then, I thought you were prettier than a seven-layer, double dutch chocolate cake. This view is much more interesting, all planes and hollows and muscles—quivering muscles. I think you're beautiful," she managed finally, and giving in to the ultimate feeling of being a woman.

Birk's hand stroked the back of her neck and wandered down to cup her breast, his thumb stroking the tip. "Finished looking?"

"Are you finished quivering?" she returned, teasing him. "I thought you'd be much heavier. There's so much to you." She rubbed the soles of her feet over his calves, luxuriating in the sturdy feel of him. She'd have to find a way to tell him—in a gentler way—that all the functional framework, from head to toe, was packaged nicely.

"Live weight weighs less and I'm not a blanket." Birk groaned and eased deeper, the movement of muscle and skin sliding against her own, a part of her and yet separate, locked together and taking away her breath. He took her chin in his hand and whispered, "Open your eyes, Lacey the lovely, and let the world spin by us."

Birk began to move and finding the unfamiliar rhythm as he waited for her, Lacey pitted herself against him, took and gave, and held him just as tightly as she could. She threw herself into the heat and storms and knew that Birk would be with her. Stars danced across her lids, flashes of summer heat mixed with thunder, and Lacey drew it closer, hoarding it, diving into it, buttering herself with the pleasure, always taking her higher. She'd lived by her wits, but now her body took her, throbbing, splintering, flying free through fire that came at her in waves, each more fierce than before.

"Lacey!" Birk's shout was lost in her own as they went soaring, plummeting, slowing through space. Lacey flung back her head, hoarding the beauty, the pleasure rolling over her. There was Birk, fierce and desperate, his eyes restless smoke, cut by primitive lightning, as he came pouring into her.

Lacey swallowed, in tune with her body, the slowing race of her pulse, and the terror that Birk would leave, taking the beauty with him.

Instead he folded magnificently, gently upon her, his head upon the pillow next to hers, dragging at air, as if he'd climbed a cliff straight up to the sky and had flopped at the summit, having given the best of himself.

She squirmed comfortably beneath him. At that summit and he'd given her the best. It was no small thing for him, it seemed, as now he seemed wasted and boneless and strangely vulnerable and endearing. Lacey smiled and smoothed his chest, testing the rapid hammering of his heart. She shifted slightly, aware of their damp skins, of Birk lying half off her, his eyes dazed slits and barely focused. "You look like a landed trout," Lacey murmured and patted his bottom.

He opened one lid and groaned as if the effort had cost him dearly.

She studied him, eye to eye on the pillow, smoothing his rumpled hair. "That wasn't so bad. Good old Birk, I can always depend on you to make things interesting. Of course, not carrying around all those muscles and pounds, I'm in much better shape than you are." Lacey sat up and shook her hair. She was energized and ready to begin a running summary of the event. She curled her arms around her legs and looked back at him, over her shoulder.

"Interesting?" Both lids were open now, though Birk hadn't moved, and the heat washing from him to her, jarred. The tension in her had burst, flinging her high, yet already it had begun simmering again at his look, begging to be let free.

He ran a hand up her back, took her hair in his fist, and drew her slowly down to his chest. "Are you all right?"

Lacey snuggled down to him, certain that he needed the rest. "It wasn't so bad."

His hand stopped smoothing her hair, fingers rubbing her scalp in that old calming way he'd used when she was a girl. "More," she whispered, arching against his hand and smoothing her hand across his chest, flowing over the hard sheathed muscle, the crisp texture of hair, the shape of this man she'd known forever and had taken to her body. He cuddled her against him, his hard thigh flexing as she rubbed hers against him. He responded so nicely to the nip on his nipple, to the dip of her tongue in his ear.

"More of what?" Birk asked above her head, the tension in his body curling around her, igniting the banked heat within her. "Oh, no," Birk protested as she slid on top of him. He held her away from him, braced his body from hers, and ran a fingertip under her eyes. "Baby, you haven't eaten all day. Elspeth dropped over with a casserole, laced with the herbs you like. She's been worried about you. Sybil sent her potato soup, and Talia sent something green and leafy. Then Alek called, and so have my brothers. I've been given strict instructions on the care and feeding of Lacey Tallchief."

Lacey slowly looked down the length of Birk's hardening body, thinking of other menus she'd rather explore. "You're worried about mauling me, bruising me, and whether we're matched evenly, and whether I'll leave you in my dust."

Birk laughed outright, the sound wrapping her in pleasure. "Tell me you don't ache."

"I'm not going to be distracted." How like Birk to stand in the way of what she wanted. Lacey stopped in the selfish thought, wrapped it around her, wallowed in it like golden sunlight. "I'll give you a reprieve."

"Mmm." He toyed with her hair, wrapping a ringlet

around his finger. The steady beat of his heart beneath her cheek had shifted into a fast shuffle, telling her that he wasn't as calm as he seemed. Tallchiefs were like that, Lacey decided, hiding their storms, but she knew that Birk wanted her now, despite his, "We could cuddle after you eat. We haven't done much of that, and—"

Lacey licked her lips and slid over him again, his body familiar on a new, exciting level. While Birk wanted to protect her, she saw no reason not to tip the scales in favor of her surprising need for him. "Rules? You know how I love to break them."

Nine

The first week of November, Lacey's virginity and her mother were gone. On her first Saturday morning as a non-virgin, Lacey moaned as she shifted through the layers of sleep. She stretched luxuriously and stopped in midarch, the new twinges of her body unexpected and uncomfortable.

A long length of hard muscled thigh rubbed roughly against her own, and Birk grumbled in his sleep.

She lowered carefully to the rumpled sheets and scanned the room. Walls weren't so bad, not when they enclosed her with Birk. Her spiffy new negligee was tossed over the old rocker, a strap from the black satin bra escaped the pillows and blankets on the floor. Something looped around her ankle and subtracting the known elements from the beginning ones, she decided Birk's shorts had somehow attached themselves to her. She eased her foot from the restriction, just as she'd always done from anything that confined her. She'd slept with Birk before, when her mother

was in the house, cuddled against him and this was no
different—

Deep in her body, tiny muscles told her that nothing
would be sweet and innocent again, not where Birk Tallchief was concerned. He had everything on his side, while
in most games between them, she knew the rules. She'd
merely beaten him in a race, once more. Or had she? Lacey
forced herself to breathe quietly. She'd frightened herself,
locked to Birk with every ounce of her strength, pitting
herself against him, against her hunger. The violence, the
driving need surged out of her and writhing on the pinpoint
of desire, she had— Lacey inhaled sharply, and squeezed
her eyes closed, remembering how Birk's back had surged
beneath her clawing hands, like waves of molten steel. She
heard the sounds again—the hard mating of their bodies,
flesh pounding flesh as if skin had burned away and they
were one body and racing heart. Throughout their lovemaking time, Lacey had not spared Birk, but yet he'd been
carefully patient with her, following her lead—which
wasn't like Birk, when he wanted.

Lacey groaned, her muscles protesting. She'd devoured
him…taken him for herself, and claimed him.

He'd been tender; she'd tasted the banked hunger inside
him and made for it, leaping over his gentle resistance,
raking him close to her, locking those long strong legs to
hers, and tossing away any inhibitions as he whispered
those dark words to her, delighting her, unshaken by her
desperation. It was as if she'd gotten Christmas all in one
big long streamlined, broad-shouldered, narrow-hipped and
long-legged, mind-blowing kissing, unexpected male surprise.

Warmth moved up her throat to heat her cheeks. She'd
set a primitive pace, leaving him no room for retreat, capturing, raiding him, and throughout the fierce rising passion—yes, passion, she clarified—she'd stepped into passion and let it burn her without a care.

Birk had let her have him; something was definitely

*wrong. She'd seen Birk romance women; he'd always been
in pursuit—definitely in charge, and very skilled.*

She'd staked him out and—

Lacey shuddered, remembering the unexpected violence
within her, and Birk's tenderness. She'd shed every tiny
speck of pride and had run him down, despite his mild
protest, and bagged him. If he acted restrained, Lacey
hadn't.

She shuddered again, afraid to face Birk, because she
knew he'd be shocked at how badly she'd wanted him.
She'd tossed ladylike and feminine out the window and
dived right for him, greedy for a brush of his lips, hoarding
the sound of his breathing, the pace of it quickening, slowing....

She dug her fists into the rosebud-splattered sheets and
stiffened as her body protested. She bit back the groan that
came curling up her throat.

There in her passion, he'd freed her somehow, burned
away her fears, and she'd been gloriously aware of how
strong she was, how feminine and desired. She'd reveled
in her capture of Birk Tallchief.

Beneath the warm nest of blankets and the cove of Birk's
body against her, his hand inched slowly upward to her
breasts, caressing them. Then his touch skimmed lower,
rubbing her stomach and lower yet to cup her. "Still feeling
cocky, Mrs. Tallchief?"

Lacey lay very still, her body leaping to heat with the
stroke of his fingers, the warm seeking of his lips along her
throat. "That wasn't fair."

He kissed her stiff shoulder. "Baby, once on your first
night is enough. There will be—"

"No more one-sided rule making. We've always been
fair with each other. I wanted you and you—"

Birk grinned, his hair tousled from sleep and her fingers.
He let her flounder and pick her way through her desire for
him. "You could help here," she muttered, with the feeling
that he'd let her stalk out on a dangerous ledge and that he

wasn't living up to his part of their usual arguments. *Something was very wrong.*

"I love that shade of blush on you. You can have me again, if you want, but I'm going to feed you first. We'll—" Birk shot her look that jarred, taking away her breath. The tenderness in his expression melted, tangled, enchanted her.

His kiss ran lightly around her lips. "Thank you, sweetheart." He curled close to her, his face nuzzling the curve of her throat and shoulder. He lay against her as though he trusted her with his life, his heart. The gentle, friendly stroke of his fingers was more potent, more seductive than a caress.

Terror skipped through Lacey. She couldn't have Birk depending on her to live up to—to what, to his expectations of a wife? Her hand hovered, tempted by his hair, by the need to stroke and comfort him.

What would she know about comforting Birk... about taking care of him, protecting him, cherishing him, as wives usually did?

Lacey frowned at the old chair, gleaming rich and beautiful beneath the scraps of lace.

The quiet moment with Birk lying against her, stroking her hip, this time without desire, but as though he enjoyed the feel of her next to him, as though she were a part of him—

The awakening, Una had called it. *When the man comes calling softly, when he places himself in a woman's care, needing the softness within her. Then she awakes, cherishing the gentleness he shows only to her—*

Lacey carefully placed her hand on his hair, smoothing it, an experiment to walking on the tender side of her emotions. His hair was sleek, warm and as familiar to her as the rain that began playing on the window. She followed the streaks down the windowpane and the desperation, the confusion eased. She was just where she wanted to be, with Birk's breath coming on her skin as steady as his heartbeat against her breast, his hand stroking her hip.

"We overslept," she murmured against his hair, enjoying the warm steely slide of his skin against hers as he lifted to peer at the bedside clock.

He flopped down beside her, running a lazy hand down her thigh. "It's only ten-thirty on a rainy Saturday."

The curve of his mouth said that Saturday spread out before them, hours of lovemaking to be filled. She never slept in, never took naps. "I never sleep in—"

"You put in overtime last night, sweetheart. You always did go for breaking the rules your first time. I'll have to work faster, Lacey the lovely, to keep up with you." A smile slid through his voice. "Do you have any idea how it feels to be zapped when I had planned to work up to the event? You've just ruined the master plan."

"Mmm?" She wanted to linger there in the quiet dim room, filled with the scents of their lovemaking, with Birk's morning stubble a slight friction on her skin, and the rain pattering on the windowpane. Rooms and walls weren't so bad, not with Birk nearby and looking at her as if he'd never get tired of the view. As if he wanted to explore her all over again; as if he found her fascinating.

Birk skimmed her body, settled the weight of his hand comfortably over her breast, caressing the softness leisurely. "There you were, all buttered and looking sexy. As the male, I'm supposed to—"

He cursed at the sound of the front doorbell, shot a dark hot look down at her, and impatiently searched the blankets for his undershorts. He paused, his hand around her ankle, to study her foot. Then with his eyes locked on hers, her heart flopping wildly in her chest, Birk lifted her foot and slowly, slowly placed his lips around her toe. He sucked gently and the heat moved from her toe slowly upward.

"You can't do that," she managed, shocked as an answering warmth flooded her.

"Can't I?" Before releasing her, Birk's big hand roamed upward, a possessive caress. He stood to pull up his shorts and his jeans, and the dim light fell around him. Across his shoulders and midway down his back, red lines laid across the rippling muscle.

She'd hurt him. Horrified, Lacey had never hurt anyone in her life, except to defend herself. "Birk, I—"

Turning to the sound of her gasp, Birk frowned. "Lacey, don't—"

As Talia called out, Birk knelt on the bed, took her face in his hands and drew her up to him. The blankets slid down and Birk's gaze shot downward, latching to her breasts and lower. "You're beautiful. Perfect. What happened between us is as natural as babies coming into the world, as daffodils coming in the spring. There's no shame in wanting me, Lacey, and in me wanting you. I just thought it would come differently to us, with me chasing you, and you battling me every inch of the way. I planned to seduce you, Lacey, my love, and lure you into my web."

He kissed her hard and hungrily, leaving her with the taste of him on her lips as he went to answer the door. Lacey gathered the bedclothes to her, shaken by the marks of her violence, her need of him.

Una's rocker gleamed in the dim light, the tiny streams on the windows coursing shadows over the old wood Birk had cleansed and prepared to last.

In the other room, Duncan laughed outright, and Megan squealed. Kira, Talia and Calum's baby, mewed and stopped suddenly as though she were nursing. Elspeth spoke quietly and Alek let out a quick laugh. Sybil, a genealogist, was muttering about her difficult socialite client and her nonexistent missing ancestor. Marcella Portway was certain that she had descended from Spanish royalty and that Sybil could find the link. All of the steady talk was familiar names, places, events.

Shaken by the new, raw, tangled emotions, by Birk's fierce, demanding kiss that told her more would come when they were alone, and by the Tallchiefs' making themselves at home, Lacey decided to dive under the covers and wait until her world settled again.

Birk laughed aloud, and the scent of freshly made coffee

seduced her. She groaned and flipped back the covers and
leaped from the bed as she usually did. She stopped in
midstep and groaned, then carefully made her way to their
clothes and dressed in her jeans and the familiar warmth
of Birk's worn flannel shirt. She smoothed the bed, no easy
task as it looked like a battleground, and ran a brush
through her hair.

One look in the mirror told her that the world would
know what had happened on the bed. Lacey shivered, and
quickly grabbed a band to secure her hair on top of her
head, hoping for an innocent teenager look. She frowned
at the mirrored image—kiss-swollen lips, cheeks flushed as
though she were still high on sex, and eyes that— Lacey
leaned closer to inspect her face. Mysterious, shaded,
heavy-lidded eyes, the shade of dark blue velvet stared back
at her. She tried for an innocent, who-me look and the
sultry image flirted back.

Lacey stuffed the negligee and lace beneath the pillows,
fluffed them, concealing the evidence. The Tallchiefs were
in her home and she had to face them. She'd never hesitated
to join them on a Saturday morning, and now she wanted
to return the welcome. She inhaled, braced herself and
jerked open the door.

They were seated around the long heavy table that Birk
had refinished, protesting her tiny round table. Heavily
built, the planks were scarred with time, and perfect for the
family that sat around it on a rainy Saturday morning. Sybil's freshly baked cinnamon rolls, mixed with the scent of
coffee curled around her. Sybil sat on Duncan's lap, his
hand on her rounded belly, smoothing it. Talia's blond hair
gleamed in a heavy braid. Her black Hessian boots were
across Calum's lap, his hand resting on her thigh, as she
nursed Kira. Alek, looking like a gypsy with an earring in
his ear, had his arm around Elspeth. Emily, a teenage red-
head and Duncan's stepdaughter, munched on a fat cinnamon roll, licking her fingers.

Thorn, Duncan's half wolf, lay at the door. Olaf, Talia's
black scarred breed lay beside Gizmo, the dogs paired for

size, and allowing the cats to snuggle close. Kira suckled noisily, her glossy black head nestled against Talia's pink sweater.

Down in Amen Flats, people were shopping, and Maddy was preparing for a Saturday night at the Hot Spot. The sheriff would be in his office, playing his opera tapes loud enough to be heard on the street.

Yet everything had changed.

She had changed.

Lacey found Birk immediately, her senses leaping, her body instantly recognizing his. He braced a foot on one chair and bounced Megan on his knee. She squealed, reaching out to Lacey, and Birk caught her, propping her on his hip, his gray eyes, the color of mist and rain on steel, locked to Lacey. He handed Megan to Emily, and leaned back against the counter, without offering her an ounce of kindness. To reach the security of his arms, she'd have to walk to him, aching from the night before.

"I'm glad you came," she managed to the Tallchiefs, certain that her lips were still swollen and rosy from his kisses...that her guilt was pasted on her face. She hovered against the bedroom door, ready to plunge back into its safety. The grim set of Birk's jaw and the arrogant lift of one brow set the steel in her spine. She wouldn't have him thinking he'd gotten the best of her. Forcing herself to move lightly, only too conscious of the unexpected heaviness of her breasts, the new intimate tingling, and the ache of her muscles, Lacey managed a weak smile.

"We're in town for Saturday groceries, and I wanted to give you this," Elspeth said, smoothing the sack labeled with her business trademark. "You have the kilt and plaid, but this is for you, a gift from a sister."

"A sister," Lacey repeated, swimming in her emotions.

"Aye," Elspeth murmured as Lacey gently eased the soft pale wool from the sack. "From Tallchief sheep. My own dear sister. You would have come to us much earlier, if Mother had her way."

"She's going to cry, and so am I," Sybil murmured softly.

"Me, too," Talia added with a sniff.

Duncan, Calum, and Alek all straightened, males alert to the disaster a woman's tears could bring. They frowned at Birk, who set his jaw and continued to stare at Lacey, expecting something from her that she didn't know how to give. She gripped the soft luxurious wool like an anchor; Birk hadn't moved.

Lacey glared though her tears at Birk, who looked as immovable and timeless and western as Tallchief Mountain. "I'm going to cry," she whispered, threatening him, because the Tallchief males were known to be susceptible to tears and the other brothers would leap to her defense.

Birk shot them a staying look, like a gunslinger ordering watchers to stay out of the way of flying bullets. "This is between us."

"My, my. He sounds like you, Duncan," Sybil purred.

"Calum has that same tone," Talia noted.

"He's bristling nicely," Elspeth offered, experienced with her own husband.

Alek, who'd had to dive into the Tallchiefs, snag Elspeth from her brothers' protection and marry her, said, "I know the feeling."

Lacey stared at them. She'd seen the Tallchief couples battle, but she'd never been inside the fighting circle. She was one half of her marriage, and feeling liberated by last night. Birk was totally susceptible to her on a level she loved. She tested her new power with one sniff and allowed the tear burning her lids to trail down her cheek, plopping on his flannel shirt.

Oh, damn, Birk thought, weakening as Lacey braced herself, looking small and delectable with her hair tumbling wildly from on top of her head and drowning in his shirt. So much for making her come to him, actually placing her arms around him, and settling his ripped pride.

They'd been too busy, meeting their work demands, and

preparing to look like newlyweds to her mother, and he hadn't done the running—

He hadn't wined and dined Lacey and made her feel comfortable as his ladylove.

Comfortable? The tiny knives slashing his pride had little to do with pleasure. Lacey had come after him on her busy schedule, skipped the ritual he had just discovered that he needed to feel secure. He'd always thought of himself as a modern male, able to handle what females threw at him, but he wasn't. Not with Lacey, not by far. She'd put him on her schedule, mop up this, and finish that, and had him, right after finishing her payroll checks. Lacey was the only woman who had left him feeling delicate and uncertain. He'd wanted to sort out what was between them, ease the change of rivals and tormentors to a different level, and time had run against him. She deserved courting and romance and flowers.

He hadn't given her a bouquet of flowers; they hadn't had one date, one romantic evening where he cooked for her and wooed her.

He wasn't up to par.

Now, since the bad-girl wrapper had come undone, she was experimenting with her sensuality. Experimenting with a look, with him.

He could handle that, since her look was for him alone, but he had to have something in return, something whimsical and delicate, and lasting as sunsets and dawns. He wanted what his parents had, and his siblings, and he wanted that for Lacey, too. She'd given him a night, not a lifetime commitment. "Come here," he said, tossing away everything he wanted, his pride demanded, but the need to hold her close.

In two steps, he had her, lifted her in his arms and sat with her on his lap.

"That's better," Lacey stated smugly, and snuggled back against him.

"Much better," Elspeth agreed and glossing over the

tense moment, nodded to the new boards, framing the future small room. "What are you building over there?"

"A nursery. Close to the main room, easy access, close to our bedroom," Birk rapped out, his gaze locked to Lacey's.

She took it like a blow, shoving free of him to stand. She stepped through the boards that would support the wall. She crouched, easing back the blanket covering a small scarred cradle, heavily laden with varnish.

Birk inhaled uneasily...the cradle was another thing that he hadn't had time to do before Lacey was ahead of him. Her fingers wandered over the cradle. Familiar with the Tallchiefs' family legends, she whispered, "It's a cradle Tallchief created and sold to support his family. A nursery. A cradle. Una's rocking chair—

The maiden who rocks upon the chair and sings a lullaby will claim the man of Fearghus blood who stands closet to her...."

She stared at Birk, and a thought hummed between them, because she had been a "maiden" until last night; she'd definitely claimed him.

Birk inhaled, sensing Lacey's rising terror. She knew the Tallchief legends, familiar with his family; she sounded as if she had been trapped and the walls were closing in—

Alek cleared his throat. "Elspeth and I have to be going."

Within minutes, Birk and Lacey were alone, and Lacey looked hunted, stricken and too pale. She hurried to the table, sloshed coffee into a mug and drank it quickly.

"That's hot. Drink slower," Birk muttered, running his hands through his hair.

"Cut the big brother act. I can take care of myself." Lacey began to pace through the house, her herd following her. She stalked to the unfinished nursery, glanced at the cradle and then scowled at Birk. "You can't be serious."

She will be his heart and he will be her love.

"I am," Birk stated curtly. He was raw inside, bleeding, and pride kept him from spreading his dreams before her.

Lacey's hands locked to the counter behind her hips. "I see. You've decided to take me up on that baby-making idea—yes, yes…that would fit right into the schedule…I mean…"

Birk moved through the distance separating them and braced his hands on either side of her. He recognized the defiant angle of Lacey's chin, the churning blue storms in her eyes, hiding her fears. "Not exactly. You skipped what I had planned. We haven't had time to sort out the rules, Lacey, but here they are—while you're my wife, you'll keep to my bed. And that goes two ways, no matter how many women you think I've known, or how badly you think my glands need servicing. I was prepared to court you, to—"

"As in date me?" Lacey sounded shocked.

Birk allowed himself a grim smile. "As in romance you, darling. You know, the long slow walks, holding hands, bundling up before the winter fire, rolling in the hay at the barn and—"

"Who are you?" she asked hesitantly, stunning him.

"You've known me all your life. You've been nothing but trouble from the day I pulled you up from that tricycle wreck. There you were with a trike too large and dangerous and fighting the world." He realized he was yelling. "I hate yelling. You're the only woman who I've ever yelled at."

His liaisons had been with women who weren't maidens and who knew what he wanted. He glared down at Lacey, barely up to his chest, with her hair in ringlets over her head and tumbling down and tendrils slipping down her nape. "I'm not your damned brother."

She sent him a look beneath her lashes, jolting him. "Maybe I like big, large dangerous bikes now."

"You've got a Harley—" Birk stopped and blinked because Lacey was smiling tremulously at him. She was trying to flirt with him and he had a sudden premonition that she was just beginning to experiment. If she tried that soft kitten appealing look with another man—

She touched his cheek, and he tumbled into the clear blue of her eyes. "Don't be mad at me, Birk. Not the deep-down kind of mad."

"No more sex, until we've worked this out," Birk stated, shaken by her quiet plea. "You can't just come home with your sack of drugstore goodies and seduce me at the end of your list of to-dos."

Lacey inhaled, scanning his face. "Birk, you mean last night was all there was? But I think I like sex with you. You're so manageable and warm and big and—"

"I'm not a playground. I'm not a blanket. I'm sensitive," he returned in a snap that jarred his teeth. "I want more."

"What do you want?" she asked, her breath warm and seductive on his lips.

He wanted a lifetime of her, babies, whispering, sharing in the night, smelling her scent and wallowing in love. The word *love* had terrified her at their reception; he wasn't coming near it again until she better understood. He'd lick his wounds and paste himself together and wait for her. "More. I'm moving out until this is settled. You can't have me without the rest, the hand-holding part, the candlelight and flowers, and long talks in front of the fireplace. And take note, Lacey the lovely, this is between us. You play games with another man and—"

"And? You won't hurt me, I know that. You had every chance last night and you—you were so tender, Birk. I never knew anything could be so beautiful. What else could you want?"

He almost felt sorry for her as she floundered, trying to understand the relationship he wanted, he had to have from her.

The dim light caught the ringlets high over her head, tumbling through the silky mass and framing her pale face. "This isn't like the other times you've yelled at me. Your roar is too quiet. I've hurt your feelings. I'm sorry."

"I'll recover." Birk scraped up his pride and pushed away from the counter before he could kiss her with the desperation raging through him. If he kissed her, he'd carry her to the bed and keep her there.

They'd exhaust each other, and begin again, without anything settled between them. While spending the day with Lacey in bed appealed, it was a patch and not a solution.

Lacey took a step toward him and paused, frowning. "I—"

Birk closed his eyes and shook his head. He strode to the bathroom, ran the big tub full of warm water and frothy bubbles and returned for Lacey, carrying her back to the bathroom. He stripped her quickly, grimly, and dumped her into the tub. Water sloshed over the side. Then because the feel of her skin, her scent had him drooling, Birk knew in another minute he'd be in the tub with her, his body already hard.

They'd end up in bed with her testing her new status as a sexual athlete. She was the first woman to cut essentials, something Birk was very careful about; they hadn't used protection, because Lacey had raced on, catching him in the agile storm of soft limbs and softer sighs and leaving him in her wake. She could be carrying his child now—a burst of reality shattered the light-headed dream, because Birk wanted Lacey to understand that he loved her.

He'd planned to spend the morning easing into the new intimacy with her—no construction crews yelling at him, no rushed schedules, just slow talk of an intimate variety, constructing a good foundation for more of the same.

She had him reeling now, plowing through his dreams like she'd power saw through boards.

She looked up at him now, the bubbles frothing around her breasts, licking at them. Her flushed cheeks were warm, a contrast to her eyes, shadowed by what she'd discovered in her sexual safari with him. The tiny scrape marks on her throat and lower reminded him of his own need as her curious gaze strolled down his body. "You were never an easy person, Birk Tallchief. Now I know why your engagements never worked out, while you had to date everyone in the countryside, until I was the only one left. I don't see why you have to be difficult about this. We have a contract. It was a necessary, make-do— I see now how vulnerable I was then and I appreciated your support. But my mother is gone now, and we are fine."

"Just *fine?*" The word chilled him, then lit his temper and shredded his dreams. They'd made love and he'd given a part of himself to her keeping that he'd given no other woman. He'd given his heart.

"Fine." No more, no less. No commitment. No dreaming between them. No intimate relations—yes, that was what he wanted, an intimate relation, more than sex. She tilted her head to one side, regarding him. "You know, you look just like Calum and Duncan do when they are really upset. They just stare, all tall and looming, and smoky-eyed. Does that throbbing vein in your temple hurt—?"

Birk pushed her head underwater, hauled her up, and used his kiss to brand her lips. He spared her nothing, just the raw primitive ache that drove his hunger for her. He eased her mouth away and nipped her bottom lip. "Take that and stick it in your 'fine' drawer."

While she was blinking and gasping and heating, Birk pushed her underwater again, scraping up what little pride he had and tucking it into his duffel bag with his clothes.

Ten

"Let me get this straight, Lacey," Talia said, after wiping away her tears of laughter. "This is better than Thanksgiving dinner coming next week, and you know how I love to eat." She glanced around Maddy's Hot Spot and the women enjoying Tuesday Ladies' Night. Talia leaned closer because Patty Jo Black—a ranch wife with sultry husky tones—was revved up at the piano doing a loud rock and roll number with Eleanor Franks, a woman with five kids and who knew how to raise the level on loud.

Maddy, a beefy giant and the only male, chewed a lollipop, and wore a battered T-shirt over his tatoos. He breezed by with a tray of mugs and a teapot of hot lemonade punch. The gong rang, signaling that an offender to the no smart children stories or kitchen recipes had been caught. Nancy Freelander stood up with her small chalkboard and ran a line through the four sticks on it. "Limit!" a woman yelled. "Nancy, one more offense and you can't come next week!"

Matilda Daniels joined Patty Jo and Eleanor, bracing her

bongo drums between her legs and began pounding away, her head bouncing to the rhythm of the loud music. The other women, including the librarian who had been circling Maddy, began to clap, hoot and stomp their feet.

Outside, the sheriff prowled by in his official car. He turned up his beloved Italian tenor squad, broadcasting the opera to Amen Flats. He knew his wife was within the territorial boundaries of Ladies Only Night, and the tenors were his way of courting her. Dogs began to howl and his wife hurried to the door. "Go home!" she yelled.

Elspeth and Sybil, both elegant women, leaned closer to hear what news Lacey had just flopped on the table. A woman who traveled through life alone, Lacey wasn't used to girl-talk, but now needed advice. A powwow of the Tall-chief women seemed appropriate.

"Birk moved out," Lacey yelled, the bongos running through the sound of the loud clapping and singing. "We were married for three weeks before we made love—actually I...I made love to him. He's too careful and I wanted— Well, one taste and he was gone. It's been two weeks."

Lacey was horribly aware that the music had stopped and her news had just been loudly broadcast to the entire gossip section of Amen Flats. Every eye in the place sighted down on her.

"Birk Tallchief waited past his wedding night to make love to you?" Patty Jo Black called from the piano, disbelief in every word.

Just at that moment, Birk jerked open the Hot Spot's door, surveyed the quiet, stunned women and found Lacey. There was nothing sweet in his unshaven appearance, his gunslinger eyes, mere slits of steel beneath his western hat. Dressed in a winter shearling coat with a turned-up collar, he was all Westerner, from leather gloves to boots. The object of Lacey's loud announcement to the women of Amen Flats sighted Lacey and scowled. "Just wondered if you were in here. Since you are, I'm leaving."

She leaped to her feet, heart pounding at the sight of

him. "It's Ladies' Night. You're not welcome," she shot at him out of habit, and wished she hadn't.

Birk's smile was cold. "Ladies, have a good time," he said smoothly, taking off his hat to tip it in the standard western greeting. A chorus of women sighed dreamily.

He stepped outside, the plastic roses on the tables quivering as he slammed the door behind him. The women looked at Lacey. "Go after him, honey," Eleanor called.

Because it was an easy exit to an embarrassing situation, Lacey nodded. She had no intention of running after Birk when she wasn't certain what he wanted. She'd go home and cry as she had been doing for the last two weeks. She'd sigh and groan and lug whatever of Birk she could find into his big empty bed. "Yes, of course, I'll just do that."

It was only the middle of November now and the winter stretched, long and cold and empty, before her.

Sybil, Talia and Elspeth grabbed her coat and pulled her back down to her seat. "Don't," they said in a collective statement as the music began again. The women of Amen Flats did not waste time on their only-female night out.

"There goes the annulment. You'll have to keep him now," Talia stated with a grin.

"I'm mad," Lacey said. "You know how this looks, with him leaving me after one night. Everyone knows, too. They know he's taken that old trapper's place at the foot of the mountains, just behind my place. People look at me and shake their heads. Birk is not the easy, laughing ladies' man they think. Oh, women may wilt when he passes, but he's got a nasty temper and he yells. I am going after that ill-mannered, poor-tempered—"

"Try lone wolf. He's acting like one, all holed up in that old cabin. Other than working until he drops, he's only stopped long enough to buy that land behind you and get groceries. I understand from gossip that in the time you've been apart, my brother is too quiet, leaves work immediately and refuses the casseroles and soups brought to his doorstep and to work."

"They take food to that old trapper's cabin behind my

place? Right past my house and down the lane to that old cabin? You know he's planted himself just miles from me, back in the timber behind Lil's, don't you? Who is cooking for him?'' Lacey asked, her heart pounding in her throat.

"Just every single woman in town and a few of the married ones,'' Talia noted. "He bought that land, by the way. I'd say he's camping on your doorstep…he hasn't wanted land before, other than the interest he holds on the Tallchief land, but he wanted that cabin, enough to pay twice what it's worth.''

"I thought those lights going down the road at night were kids, necking—'' Lacey fought leaping to her feet, running out to her pickup and setting up a roadblock to her husband.

Elspeth adjusted her shawl, an elegant movement of her artistic hands. "My brother is probably licking his wounds. You looked shocked, ready to faint when he told you he was building a nursery and you found the Tallchief cradle.''

"I didn't know he was so…delicate,'' Lacey moaned, smoothing the small lump beneath her sweater. She cherished the agate, the leather thong holding it, and everything Birk had left in her care—except Birk, who couldn't step over his pride to come back to her. "I feel like I'm working without a blueprint and I've never liked not understanding the rules,'' Lacey muttered.

"Could I have Birk?'' Marcy James called, teasing.

Lacey glared at Marcy. "He's taken, sweetie.''

"It's a family secret that my brothers are fragile, not delicate,'' Elspeth stated wisely.

Lacey propped her boots onto the table, ready to brood about Birk. "Birk has never been fragile with me. Since I was seventeen, it has been out-and-out war. He hung my jacket on a high hook once, with me in it. What about all the times he threw me in the lake?''

"Things have changed between you, a natural change. Maybe you should have this talk with him, when you're both calm. But not now—you'd accomplish nothing,'' Sybil said.

"'Calm' might not be possible," Elspeth offered. "They've been battling for years and looking back, I think it was all coming down to this. Lacey, you are coming to Thanksgiving dinner, aren't you?"

"Not if Birk is going to be there. The way I'm feeling now, I could throw that entire stuffed turkey at him. He's embarrassed me."

"Don't dump gravy on him, either. Wear something feminine instead," Talia suggested. "And Calum once hung my jacket on a hook, with me in it. Look where we are now." She glanced down at her burgeoning, milk-filled breasts. "I hope I left enough milk for Kira in the refrigerator."

Lacey mentally circled her clothing wardrobe. Birk had always dated very feminine women, who dressed— She looked at her paint-splattered boots. "I have my black leather skirt and red sweater set—"

Talia patted her hand. "Very nice. But I was thinking more of something softer, sweeter, more bridelike. And when he snarls, try fluttering your lashes and smiling with allure. By the way, Birk had coffee with Calum the other day. Birk poured milk into his coffee and looked so low and alone and brooding, while Calum was going over his accounts, that I didn't have the heart to tell him it was mother's milk."

"So much for allure," Lacey muttered as she stood outside the small cabin, dressed in her long woolen overcoat that reached her snow boots. Winter whipped her coat around her bare legs and she missed her long thermal underwear. After Thanksgiving dinner Birk had talked with everyone else, played with the children, and then excused himself without one look at Lacey. Unapproachable, except to everyone else, Birk hadn't spared her a look and her brand-new expensive, gauzy rosebud skirt and matching sweater had been wasted.

"We are married, after all." Lacey threw a snowball at Birk's window. The small one-room cabin was an old hid-

ing place, one he'd rooted her out of years ago. His truck
was parked in front, and she'd seen his shadow in the window. A mountain of firewood waited, stacked outside his
door. It was probably necessary winter wood, rather than
wood harvested because he was emotional, Lacey decided.
She remembered him the night she'd come to see him, just
after his parents were killed. He was a boy then, rangy and
trying to look tough and yet so sweet when he held her on
his lap and rocked her into the night.

Birk jerked open the door, filling the space with his
broad-shouldered, rangy frame. There was nothing sweet
about him now. "What do you want?"

"I'm cold," Lacey tossed bait to him. He'd never failed
to cuddle her when she was small, to warm her. She wanted
him back in her bed, next to her. She wanted him back in
her life; she was miserable without him. She threw another
snowball and it splatted against the door he had just closed.
They'd been in thousands of snowball fights during the
years and she hoped—

He jerked the door open again. "I'm not coming out and
playing tonight, Lacey. Go home to your nice warm bed."

"Can I—?" The door was closed again and the cabin
was dark. He couldn't do that to her, Lacey decided. She
plucked the casserole she had made from the hood of her
truck, adjusted the backpack straps on her shoulders, and
tromped through the snow on her way to get her husband's
attention.

She took a deep breath before knocking on the door, and
glanced at the old ladder leaning against the cabin.

Birk sat sprawled in the dark and listened to Lacey's
imperial knock, which slid into an angry one. He tucked
away the pictures of her that he'd tacked to the wooden
logs. A world-famed journalist, but also an excellent photographer, Alek had enlarged a picture of Lacey at Elspeth's wedding, wearing her Tallchief plaids. With her hair
catching the wind, the ringlets flying high and out, Lacey
had been a part of his family as she always had. The picture

was taken just minutes before The Kiss, and she was already leaning back against Birk. Pride wasn't a thing that he'd bothered about, but now, he needed to know that Lacey cared on a different level than anything before.

Amid the Tallchiefs' Thanksgiving Day, Lacey's new feminine look had slammed into Birk with the force of a landslide. Every movement enchanted him—the sweep of her neck, the tendrils framing her face, her scent— She'd stunned him, and when she'd held Kira against her, cooing to Calum's baby—

He listened to the knock grow louder, more insistent, and tapped his boot on the wooden floor. He couldn't run out the door, haul her into his arms, and kiss her like he wanted. Lacey had always been fast and agile and way ahead of him. "I'm slower, but I'm thorough," Birk muttered as he sipped his cup of instant soup and ran his hand across his bare chest. He'd just taken his bath, washing away the sweat from his chopping fiesta. Chopping wood didn't ease the need to go to Lacey's house and have her. Birk frowned. What he wanted wasn't a one-way street, and Lacey had made it clear that she wasn't missing him. He wouldn't button his shirt for Lacey or make anything easier for her.

The door rattled and Birk locked himself to his chair, tipped against the wall. A mitten ran across the old window, high on the wall, swiping away a thin layer of snow. A whomp sounded against the side of the cabin and a moment later, Lacey's face appeared at the window. Standing on the ladder, she couldn't see him in the shadows, but the moonlight outside outlined her head. She pushed and grunted and the window swung open. Wind and snow briefly entered the room and Birk braced himself against the next event.

Lacey eased in one leg and carefully edged through the small opening, taking care of the object in her hand. Her boot found a chair and Lacey stepped onto it, closing the window after her. She agilely leaped off the chair and placed the foil-wrapped square on the table. She glanced at the back door, muttered to herself on the way to it, jerked it open and yelled, "Run away, you...you husband. I knew you couldn't take it."

She slammed the door, and jerked off her mittens and cap. She was on her way to her boots when Birk allowed the front two legs of his chair to hit the floor.

"You!" she whispered, her hand going to her throat. "I thought you'd left by the back door."

Birk stood and because he wanted to grab her so desperately, he forced himself to put more wood in the old stove. When his hands stopped trembling, Birk turned to her. "Just what can't I take?"

In the flickering light from the stove, she looked so small and scared that part of him wanted to gather her close and kiss away her fears.

Another part wanted her to come to him, to tell him that she loved him.

"I brought you a casserole. It's a neighborly thing to do. It's a...meat and potato casserole, a big one...I made it myself." She smoothed her hair as Birk lit the old lantern and the light spread over her. She shrugged free of the backpack, and took a plastic bowl from it, placing it on the old wooden table. "Salad," she explained. "Casseroles aren't so hard to make, just mixing up stuff in layers and baking it. I bought a cookbook."

"Nervous?" he asked and wished his stomach would quit hurting from the sight of her, all rosy and cold from the wind.

Lacey swallowed, her eyes luminous and huge, catching the light. "Birk, I...I need you. I thought we could eat dinner—the casserole needs to be warmed—"

Birk slid the warm glass pan into the small metal oven on top of his wood stove. "That takes care of that. You need me? How?" As a brother? As a friend? As a lover? Or as a combination of all and the other part of her heart? "I..."

She'd cooked for him, a unique event in Lacey's life. When contributing to the Tallchiefs' dinners, she usually brought pickles and olives, or a tray of celery sticks stuffed with cheese fillings. Birk inhaled her scent and the one that she had purchased the night of her seduction—the night of her conquest of him, he corrected. The casserole slightly appeased his restless storms and he prayed there would be more—

Lacey glanced down at her coat and her fingers fluttered over the buttons. Birk watched, fascinated. "If you're hot, you can take off your coat."

"No. I'll keep it on. I'll set the table." But she hadn't moved from where she stood, her eyes locked to his bare chest.

At least he had that from her, the tension humming in Birk's body, the need to grab her and bear her down to the bed squeezing his chest. "Did you take down the walls...the nursery?" he asked finally, needing to know.

Was she sleeping in his bed? Was she remembering how their bodies fit and heated and loved....?

"I...I finished it. Put in some shelving, painted them white. Do you think the casserole is hot enough yet?" she asked as an old plate fell from her fingers to clatter on the table. "Birk, you left all those wedding gifts—"

Correction. I left you my heart and my dreams.

He leaned against the wall and braced his boot against the bed. He hooked his thumbs in his belt, because in another minute he'd be reaching for her. "What do you want, Lacey?"

He wouldn't be swayed by her trembling bottom lip, her shy glance at him, or her color rising, the droplets of perspiration glowing on her forehead, dampening the tendrils clinging to her cheek. "Lacey, take off your coat."

"Maybe after dinner."

Impatient with her and with himself, Birk shoved from the wall and quickly unbuttoned her coat. She pushed back from him and flung open her coat, stripping it from her. "Oh, fine. You have to ruin this, I suppose—"

"You're naked," he said when he could speak. In the lamplight, she was pale and curved and gleaming, her hair flowing around her shoulders. Surprise tempered with outrage and flipped over into desire. "You'll catch pneumonia."

"I've known you all my life. Why is this so hard?" she said slowly, placing her hand on his chest and stroking the crisp hair.

She leaned against him, placing her hands on his cheeks. "You're looking so tired, Birk. There are circles beneath your eyes, and you've lost weight."

Her hands floated across his face, tracing his features, examining him as though he were brand-new to her. "I'm sorry I bricked you into that wall closet, years ago. You were sleeping so soundly and I really didn't like news of your engagement."

He kissed the palm closest to his mouth. "The mortar hadn't set yet. I dug out. You made me late for a date. Nancy wasn't understanding."

"I like touching you," she whispered, as though mulling her thoughts, balancing them. "I like kissing you."

Her fingertips floated across his lips. "Why is this so difficult?"

He kissed her fingers, suckled them one by one. "We're changing what's between us."

"I like the action, the competition. You're a good match, Birk. And not that dull. Do you think we could still have that?"

"We can have that and more."

Lacey closed her eyes and shivered. "How much more?"

Birk inhaled and gathered her against him, rocking her. "Why did you come here, dressed like this?"

"It's called allure," she whispered against his chest, her lips so soft that his skin leaped to their touch.

Birk took a step backward as Lacey gently pushed against him. "You'll have to say it, Lacey."

She studied him, her lips parted. "Let me take you ice-skating on the pond."

She wasn't giving in easy, and he respected that. He

toyed with her curls and his other hand slid down to smooth her bottom. "As in a date?"

She rested her head on his shoulder and kissed his throat. "I'll buy you flowers and call you every coffee break. We can have breakfast at the café and I'll learn to cook—"

"What about breakfast here tomorrow morning?" Birk bent to pull back the blanket and sheet from the single bed, and fused his mouth to hers.

It was a start, Lacey thought, watching her husband stride through the new school addition, bending to heft a roll of insulation and toss it against a new wall. Dressed in a battered sweatshirt, jeans and work boots, Birk looked like a warrior, proud, confident, set on his course.

He looked nothing like the tender lover of the previous night, comforting her when she cried. Lacey pushed away the tears that threatened her now. When had she first hungered for him? From the first moment he'd plucked her from the tricycle wreck?

He was impatient, scowling, using one hand to vault over an island sink in the science room. She'd seen him act like this thousands of time before. How many December firsts had come and gone, blending their lives? and now suddenly everything had changed.

She found herself thinking about him while she was checking the electrician's work, the remodeling contract almost completed. There, lying stomach down, next to the church's brand-new super-duper water heater, Lacey thought of Birk. Desperate to see him, she'd bypassed the minister, poised with another building change on his lips. She'd hurried to her pickup, aching to see Birk.

Now, breathing hard from hurrying and the biting wind, her pulse kicking up, Lacey felt her heart flip over when she saw him. Her hand went to the agate resting beneath her sweatshirt. Birk's head was turned at an angle as he listened intently to one of his men. In a gesture of frustration, he ran his hand across the back of his neck. How many times had she seen him do that familiar gesture? The next heartbeat, he frowned, turned suddenly and his eyes locked on her.

The jolt sent her reeling, tumbling back into the quiet morning hours when he'd allowed her to gather him to her, holding him on top of her when he would have moved away. That was the time she loved best, when Birk gave himself into her care, resting within her arms, vulnerable, waiting—

Who was he? she wondered as the slow heat began simmering in her, skittering along her skin with just one look from Birk.

He strode to her, still frowning. He caught her chin, tipped her face up for a hard, fast kiss, then lifted his head to study her. He searched her face and Lacey couldn't put up her barriers, couldn't tease or torment him, couldn't— couldn't...

"What's wrong?" he asked, the frown deepening, as he placed his hand on her shoulder.

She struggled to find her voice and her thoughts came out in a soft wail. "I don't know who you are." Then, because she was tripping, falling over uncharted emotions, she added, "I'm not dressed right."

She should have been wearing something feminine—

"You're dressed for work. Are you hurt?" Birk glanced down at her overalls, the sweatshirt beneath them, and down to her boots. He pivoted her around to check her backside, and turned her to him, in a deft movement she remembered from her childhood. How many times had he picked her up, dusted off her clothing and made the "bad" go away? Finding nothing, his mouth hardened. "Lacey, if your mother has called, I want you to promise me, you'll tell me."

She swallowed, drowning in questions. Now, nothing seemed important, but what happened between Birk and herself, the changes, the softening, the loving— "What are we doing? Who are you?"

Birk slowly began to smile, a devastating curve of his lips that kicked up her heartbeat and tightened her body, then skimmed along her skin, heating it. He cupped her nape and leaned closer, filling her eyes with him, her body reacting immediately. "It's not even coffee break time yet and you like schedules. You came to see me on an impulse. I like that. We're who we are. We're who we've always been and yet, more. Any more questions?"

"I...I...can't think. This is too easy, Birk. I feel too much for you, as if you—" She floundered, uncertain now of her exact feelings and not wanting to share them too soon. She hurried through her emotions, afraid of them. "You fill me...I...just the sight of you—"

"Aye, that's how it is, darling." He tugged her closer and told her with his hungry kiss that nothing would be easy with him. The fierce storm ignited in her, leaping into fire and need before she could catch it. She arched against him, her ball cap bumping his forehead, until Birk flung it away, deepening the kiss.

Lacey dived into the familiar heat, pulled him closer, this man she'd known all her life. "Come back to me," she whispered against his mouth, when they were breathless and steaming and staring at each other.

Birk tensed at Matt Doolin's yell, "The inspector is on the phone, Birk. He has questions."

Birk cursed, shot a scowl at Doolin, and drew Lacey's arms from his neck and strode away. Then in midstep, he turned, frowned at her as though he'd forgotten something. He placed a hand on a counter and swung over it in a single smooth movement, and closed the short distance to her. He cupped her chin, brushed his lips across hers and said, "By the way, I love you. I want everything, Lacey the lovely. The works."

"What do you mean?" She tried to breathe and couldn't. He couldn't love her....

"Love. I love you, darling," Birk murmured, his eyes crinkling with laughter and with tenderness.

"Birk!" Doolin yelled. "The inspector says if you don' take this call now, he'll make us wait two weeks longer fo an okay."

"Tell him he can shove—no, I will." Birk glanced down at Lacey, kissed her again and whispered, "Aye. I've hunted through swarms of women to find the best, Lacey my lovely. You're mine. You've always been. I'll be home for supper."

By the way, I love you.... You're mine. You've always been. Lacey reeled, light-headed, and repeated what Birk had just said, trying to absorb it. She closed her eyes as the legend from Una's journals circled her. *The maiden who rocks upon the chair and sings a lullaby will claim the man of Fearghus blood who stands closest to her. She will be his heart and he will be her love.*

Eleven

Birk slammed his pickup door, and gathered the ruined florist bouquet under his jacket. It was now hours past supper, closer to midnight. On the way from the florist, he had passed a wreck on the road and had stopped. After using his radio to call the sheriff, he'd tracked a dazed mother, holding her baby, down a ravine. By the time the sheriff arrived, Birk was tucking her into his truck. The florist's bouquet of red roses had gotten crushed in the process.

"I'll be home for supper," he repeated now, looking at Lacey's dark house. She deserved romance, a candlelight dinner, and sweet talk. *Then* he should have told her he loved her, when she was warm and purring in his arms. *Then,* after telling her he loved her, he should have given her the Celtic ring circling the tip of his little finger, and Una's small knife from Tallchief, and the barbaric gold band, formed by tiny Celtic designs, for her upper arm. "The works. Lacey isn't a woman who wants someone else laying out her life for her. You didn't rate high there in the romance department, Tallchief," Birk muttered.

After taking the woman to the hospital, he'd hurried to collect his inheritance from Elspeth's keeping. Sometimes, Elspeth just knew what he wanted, and had been waiting at the door with his share of Una's inheritance. She'd handed them to him without a word, but came close to kiss him. "Mother always said you'd choose a difficult love, and from the looks of you, I'd believe her. Lacey won't let you sway her with your lady killer looks and manners, Birk the rogue. She'll have you on a platter and you'll love it."

He didn't feel like the smooth-tongued lady-killer of his reputation. He wanted everything to be perfect for Lacey, and he'd slammed "I love you," at her like a trout that he'd caught and wanted her to cook. "I'll be home for supper," had come naturally from him, like the love he felt for her.

Birk averted his head against the wind and took the steps two at a time.

Lacey had looked so small, so shocked when he told her that he loved her. She'd paled and grasped an unfinished counter, looking as though he'd slapped her. He should have gone back to her, or told the inspector to— Birk scanned the house, and knew without looking further, that she was gone. He tossed the bouquet and the leather pouch with the armband and Una's knife onto the couch as he passed, undressing on his way to the shower. He was too ragged now, tired, dirty, and angry with himself...with Lacey for looking shocked. He stepped into the shower, muttering, and turned the water on hot to get the ice out of his bones. He'd get himself back together, get all his raw edges under control and then he'd track her down. Birk soaped grimly, rinsed, and stepped out of the shower, bracing himself at the scent of her. "You know the routine, Tallchief. Dinner, dancing, a few kisses, and then, then, you tell her you love her."

"I've never liked routine." Lacey was leaning against the counter, her arms crossed in front of her, and her bare foot tapping. The black scrap of lace she wore set Birk's body on alert, her hair tumbling and gleaming around her shoulders.

Birk didn't think, couldn't stop. He reached for her, wrapped his hand around her neck and dragged her against him for a hungry kiss.

Lacey shoved back, breathing hard, her cheeks flushed. A jerk of her head brought her chin up and tossed her hair behind her shoulder. "Now let me get this straight. You romance women, then you tell them you love them. Oh, don't look around for my herd to save you, Birk Tallchief. They're corralled on the back porch. You'll have to stand and fight, all by yourself."

Birk ran his hand across the back of his neck. He was too raw and fearing that she'd tell him that it was over. A fist slammed into his stomach, hiking his anger back up again. He wouldn't lie to Lacey, or try to ease what he felt for her. "I've told two women I loved them. I thought I did and was getting married at the time, so it seemed appropriate. Now, I know they were only words. I know that I've come up short when it comes to romancing you. We should have had dates, candlelight dinners, and music. I'm not a bad dancer—we've never danced together since you were seventeen. And hell, I need romance—I intend to wine and dine and dance with you for the rest of my life. I want picnics and family and snowball fights. I want to hold you at night and wake up to you in the morning. I want to fill that cradle and the nursery and the upper story with babies, if not ours then children who need us. But most of all, I want you. Do you want to argue about that?"

"So you said words that were 'appropriate'. I'll have none of that, Birk Tallchief. I'll want the real words, the ones from your deep dark savage heart, or none at all."

"You're a contrary woman, Lacey," he said, meaning it.

"So you married me to protect me from my mother, eh?" she said, making a statement, rather than a question. "I think you married me because you're just like Duncan and Calum and Alek. You saw what you wanted and an opportunity to get it. You were chased by women, flirted with them, a regular dashing Romeo, but when it came down to what you wanted, you didn't hesitate to claim me. I've thought about this, once I recovered from this morning and your little surprise.''

Birk tensed, nettled by her perception of the truth. He knew Lacey well enough not to put too much power in her hands. ''Could be.''

''So you married me because you wanted me. I can handle that...the claiming tendency you males seem to have. I've seen it happen with Elspeth, Talia and Sybil. It's instinctive, I suppose.'' Lacey licked her lips, her body seemed to soften as she turned and walked from the bathroom, glancing over her shoulder at him. The sheer black nightie swayed around her hips as she moved, flared as she turned, facing him, her legs apart and her hands on her hips. Birk tried to keep from grabbing her, and carrying her off to bed, while Lacey faced him. ''I won't wear LaBelle's ring. It's too costly. I know you got me that first job with Pop Ramirez, who thought I was too small and weak to handle it. I know you got the bank to loan me money to get started in business. I know you've told at least two women you loved them and you're never telling another one, not while I'm your wife.''

The tightness in Birk's chest eased a notch. He scooped the flowers from the couch and shoved them at her. ''Fine. Here's your bouquet.''

Oh, she'd wear LaBelle's ring, Birk thought, but he'd save that argument for another time. When she was melting beneath him....

Lacey gathered the crushed, wilting and half-frozen flowers to her, smiling softly into the petals. ''They're beautiful. I'll want wildflower ones, too. And ones from the rose garden I've always wanted. I've a notion to grow things— calves, lambs and other small, young things. You'll have to fence in the land between the house and the cabin, and you can't go there without me—at least not to sleep. You must always sleep with me, darling. There will be no more hiding in that cabin for you."

"You're a demanding woman, Lacey Tallchief. I think I can manage that." Raw desire surged through Birk, stunning him, locking his bare feet to the floor, jarring every muscle in his body.

She tossed the flowers aside, and slowly looked down his aroused body. She licked her lips and leaned back against the couch, bracing her arms against it, a seductive pose. Her foot came out to slide slowly up his leg. "Nice. But I'm not feeling sweet. What else did you bring me, Birk the rogue?"

The game was on, he thought, loving her more. She'd experiment, push him, and he'd give her everything she wanted— "There's this." He took the small, gold ring from his finger and slipped it onto hers. "It's Una's, a Celtic friendship ring, but—" Birk slid the arm bracelet high on her arm, watched the old Celtic designs glow against her skin, and the sweet curve of Lacey's lips as she turned to him.

"I'll treasure them, and you, Birk Tallchief. I've nothing to give you but my heart—no family inheritance, no loving family, absolutely nothing but my heart."

Birk inhaled, the pain easing another notch as Lacey continued, "If you only know how much I fought running you down when you were late. But I've decided on a new game. Only you or one of the Tallchiefs would have gone down that ravine after that woman. I know all about it, and I know that when it comes to caring, the Tallchiefs have always been a part of me, and I adore them. But, if you're wanting a sweet wife—" She tipped her head back and the air sizzled between them as she sent him a look and a challenge.

"You are sweet, and delicate and the most feminine woman I've known. You're also the most contrary, too independent by far and can't be trusted when it comes to playing games." Lacey was setting the rules and leaving him to battle his way through the usual to the unique, who was his wife. He slowly ran his fingers across the bow tethering her lingerie and jerked, tearing the bow apart.

"That wasn't nice, but appropriately savage, and in tune with how I feel now. Ah, Birk, you're always there when I need you," she purred with a smile that jolted his heart. She allowed the lingerie to drop to her feet and stepped out of it, drying his mouth. She arched and stretched and ran her hand down her bare hip, moving sensuously toward him. "I've put on a few pounds, here and there, and I'm not that delicate. I won't have you playing my guardian when we're making love, Birk darling. I can handle myself. We're going to have equality in this marriage."

"There's a certain amount of he-she designated duties. You've allowed for that, of course." He sighed, moving backward with each prod of her finger. He hoped he could make it to the bedroom before dragging her to him. Now Lacey was setting the rules, needing her equality in their relationship. He intended to give her so much, and then claim her. Her finger strolled down his chest, toyed with his navel and when she touched him, he jumped, tensing against the need to pull her down to the rug.

"You need to know me better, Birk darling," Lacey said, placing her hands on his chest and smoothing it, before she pushed him down on the bed. "Because when it comes to loving you— Oh, Birk, how I love you. I always have."

She fell upon him before he could shift to sweet and tender and careful...before he could put up the barriers to protect her from his strength and need.

Her kiss ravaged, stormed, fired, her hands moving over him, and his finding what he sought— There was nothing sweet or tender, rather a fierce slanting of mouths, a nibbling of lips, the heat building as Lacey straddled him, her eyes half closing as he raised high into her. The moonlight crossed into the room, caught her breasts, the pale shimmer and sway of softness that he drew into his lips, nibbling, fighting the red pounding waves as Lacey dived and plunged and took his mouth again, arching her body taut against his. Lacey cried out, matching his rhythm, gripping him tight with her body.

She was his, mating with him, creating one body, one life, one love, fighting for the ultimate release—or was it a final bonding that would last forever?

Birk, unable to curb his need, turned her beneath him, plunged into her and she cried out. He paused, shaken, fearing that he'd hurt her, and then Lacey bit his shoulder and pushed at him, again straddling him. Her hair flew around her shoulders, draping over her breasts as he cupped them, caressed them, the rhythm coming faster, hotter—

"This is what we are," she whispered, breathing hard against his shoulder.

She'd frightened herself, needing him, fighting the waves of pleasure and more riding her. She would have no gentle lover, but the raw primitive power of her husband—there would be other times, gentler times, when they would love, but this time was to burn away the past, to make them one—this was her lover, her friend, her heart, and she would have nothing less than all of him. She'd never been so strong, meeting him there in the pounding rhythm, the fierce heat devouring them. She would tell him—no, Lacey shivered, ached, forced herself to grasp his jaw, drag his wonderful mouth to hers and feed upon him.

Beneath her hands, his body was her own, her life was his. Lacey dived into the flavors of her husband, new delightful flavors, the primitive ones that he couldn't hoard from her. The first wave hit her, blinding her, driving her upward.

No easy man, this, but her wild, fierce lover.

"Birk, I love you!" The cry came from her heart, from the core of what she was and what she would be—untamed, lush and true. Reveling in the release, she gave herself to the words, wallowed in them, tossed them into the night, out high into the stars and over the moon. He had to know, had to feel how desperately she loved him.

In the shadows, Birk's eyes were light, smoking with the

heat devouring them. There was nothing civilized about him now, no laughing, easy, tender lover—his hair cut across the pillow, wild from her hands, his brows drawn and fierce and black. She wouldn't have anything less than the primitive gleam of his high cheekbones, his jaw tense and locked with desire, the sensuous curve of his mouth set for the ultimate—

Heat bloomed and stormed and hit her again and again, driving her higher and still she rode on, driving over the crest and with his name on her lips, fell softly, softly, down—

All that he was came surging out of him, spilling into her, giving her what he was and would be, and with it his promise. "I love you, Lacey my love."

She gave herself to his keeping, letting him fold her against him, stroking her shivering body, easing her slowly back down beside him. She smiled as Birk leaned to brush her lips with his, to nuzzle aside the curls and find her ear. She listened to his dark sweet words, drifting in the caress of warm big hands over her body, gentling the storm that had passed, but would leap to life soon.

Beneath her cheek, his heartbeat slowed from the wild hammering that had matched her own.

"You're mine," she whispered against his damp skin, wrapped in his arms.

"Aye, that I am," he whispered in a drowsy tone wrapped in humor and love.

Twice more in the night, he awoke, hungry for her, and she reveled in his need, in the life they would have.

In the morning, Birk was gone.

Lacey showered carefully, and smiled when she found a tender spot on her thigh. There were scrape marks on her shoulder and a tender softness around her mouth. She'd had Birk, loved him until he dropped. Her smile grew, curved around her body, warming it. He'd groaned this morning, sliding out of bed and stretching. She'd had him, well and good, and he would know it, she'd thought drifting back to sleep.

Oh, those sweet soft words he'd whispered. She'd make him pay for those, she'd learn just how to whisper in the night, because she was looking at a lifetime of surprising Birk, nudging his guard and loving him.

Then there would be the soft moments, because he needed them, and her, too. She'd have to learn how to romance him, how to dress in swishy, seductive dresses, or prim ones for church that would make him drool until they came home—

Lacey frowned and hurried to dry, pausing to study the Celtic ring on her finger and the primitive bracelet on her upper arm. There was a new softness to her body, a heaviness to her breasts, well loved in the night—oh, her husband knew how to touch her, how to love her, to please her.

His words had come raw and true, warming her, catching her in beauty, in hunger, for she had the best of Birk Tallchief, what he was, and he had what she was and would be.

Lacey ran her hands slowly over her soft bare stomach, the ring and bracelet gleaming rich and old on her pale skin. She'd heard the Tallchief wives talk, and Elspeth shared the look that— Lacey leaned closer to the mirror, lifted her hair away from her face, studied the new softness around her jaw—

A baby! She carried Birk's baby! She didn't need tests or doctors or anything but the pounding of her heart.

She trembled as she dressed in the clothing he'd laid out for her beneath the tiny sheathed knife—her thermals, Una's wedding shift, the beaded moccasins. He'd added her down jacket against the biting wind coming down from Tallchief mountain. Then she pulled the old rocker to a window, settled upon it with her hands on her stomach and waited, humming a lullaby—

Una must have waited for Tallchief in just the same way. *The maiden who rocks upon the chair and sings a lullaby*

*will claim the man of Fearghus blood who stands closest
to her. She will be his heart and he will be her love.*

She waited with her love, for her love, cherishing the
time alone and when he would come. Birk would run true
to his heritage, pleased with the baby.

He'd understand when she told him that she needed to
find her brother and sister. He'd help her and he'd be there
when she needed him.

She saw him as a boy, tending her bruises. As a man,
yelling at her. As a lover, tender and sweet, and giving
himself to her care. How many times had he placed his
face in her hands, kissing them, a complete surrender.

Lacey smiled and smoothed her stomach where she was
certain Birk's baby nestled. She was a part of her husband,
and he, a part of her, their hearts blending—though she
couldn't make it too easy for him.

A horse moved through the light snow, coming to Lil's
Place, the rider pulling a packhorse behind him.

Lacey rested a moment, treasuring the fierce pride in her
husband, who was—when all his civilization was stripped
away—a very traditional husband. He wanted their love to
be as true and fierce and strong as Una and Tallchief's, and
he would take her to his wilderness lair and they would
dine upon each other—

She stood, calm now, dressed in the heavy winter coat,
and placed the heavy, woven blanket around her. She left
the dark past, and walked outside, toward her husband and
her future.

Birk didn't welcome her with a smile, his pride fierce
and flashing in his eyes, the set of his beautiful lips. She
came closer, and looked up at him, her husband.

He lowered his gloved hand to her, and stuck out his
boot.

Lacey took his hand, stepped on his boot and Birk lifted
her easily to the saddle in front of him, adjusting the blanket carefully around her. He paused for a light kiss, giving
her that sweet moment. Love shone in his eyes, and another
kiss would serve as their vows. There would be other times

to whisper "I love you," other times for that intense heat,
soaring tempers, and for laughter and for making up. All
the rich textures waited for them, and she would tend each
one carefully, loving him.

She settled back against her husband, and let him take
her to her future.

"It's not Christmas yet," Birk said, glancing at the huge,
wrapped package in Lacey's arms. He tossed the hammer
aside, and stripped off his gloves—they'd been widening
the windows to give a better view of Tallchief Mountain.
After Sunday dinner, the Tallchief family had just left—
Sybil's baby was overdue, and Duncan was on edge, terrified that snow-filled roads would keep them from a doc-
tor.

Elspeth would be the next to have a baby, and Alek was
glowing nicely. Talia had Calum thinking about another
baby, and while he was planning and thinking, she would
probably have her way, delighting him.

Fiona, like a sister to Lacey, would be home for Christmas.

"I couldn't wait."

Birk looked at her, that quiet pleased look that took her
heart soaring. "Aye," he said, reminding her of how she
suited him. "You're blushing, Lacey the lovely. I thought
we were past that."

"Not quite. And you've blushed once or twice yourself."

He bent to kiss her. "Only when you winded me." He
lifted an eyebrow, mocking her. "You couldn't wait last
night."

"Romance takes so much time."

Birk took the wrapped package, leaned against the wall
and carefully pulled the bow away. "This is the first present
I've given you since we've been married."

"You've given me many, many presents," he reminded
her with a wicked grin.

The paper came away to a cradle board, fashioned of

willow and doeskin and fringes and beading. One of Una's five crystals snuggled in the beading that Elspeth had helped Lacey design.

Birk inhaled shakily, then let his breath out slowly. "If this is what I think it means—" He searched Lacey's face.

"It is. Sit down, Birk the beloved. I think you're going to faint."

He shook his head, eased down to the couch and wilted magnificently. She touched the tears on his lashes, kissed his nose and settled into his lap with a smile. His hand found her stomach, spreading over it and the new life they had begun. His reverent expression was beautiful, delighting her. "Come here, Birk my beloved, and let me tell you how much I love you."

In the dim winter light by the windows, the old rocking chair gleamed, creaking as a cat leaned against it.

She will be his heart and he will be her love.

*   *   *   *   *

Daniel MacGregor is at it again...

New York Times bestselling author

NORA ROBERTS

introduces us to a new generation of MacGregors
as the lovable patriarch of the illustrious MacGregor
clan plays matchmaker again, this time to his three
gorgeous granddaughters in

THE MacGREGOR BRIDES

From Silhouette Books

Don't miss this brand-new continuation of Nora Roberts's
enormously popular *MacGregor* miniseries.

Available November 1997 at your favorite retail outlet.

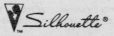

Take 4 bestselling love stories FREE

Plus get a FREE surprise gift!

SILHOUETTE® *Desire*®
15 YEARS OF GUARANTEED GOOD READING!

Desire has always brought you satisfying novels that let you escape into a world of endless possibilities— with heroines who are in control of their lives and heroes who bring them passionate romance beyond their wildest dreams.

When you pick up a Silhouette Desire, you can be confident that you won't be disappointed. Desire always has six fresh and exciting titles every month by your favorite authors— **Diana Palmer, Ann Major, Dixie Browning, Lass Small** and **BJ James,** just to name a few. Watch for extraspecial stories by these and other authors in **October, November and December 1997** as we celebrate **Desire's 15th anniversary.**

Indulge yourself with three months of top authors and fabulous reading…we even have a fantastic promotion waiting for you!

Pick up a Silhouette Desire… it's what women want today.

Available at your favorite retail outlet.

DIANA WHITNEY

**Continues the twelve-book
series 36 HOURS in
September 1997
with Book Three**

OOH BABY, BABY

In the back of a cab, in the midst of a disastrous storm,
Travis Stockwell delivered Peggy Saxon's two precious babies
and, for a moment, they felt like a family. But Travis was a
wandering cowboy, and a fine woman like Peggy was better off
without him. Still, she and her adorable twins had tugged on
his heartstrings, until now he wasn't so sure that *he* was
better off without *her.*

For Travis and Peggy and *all* the residents of Grand Springs,
Colorado, the storm-induced blackout was just the beginning
of 36 Hours that changed *everything!* You won't want to miss a
single book.